MW00936980

Last
Atonement

A Gideon Johann Western
Book 7

By
Duane Boehm

Last Atonement: A Gideon Johann Western Book 7

Copyright 2016 Duane Boehm

All rights reserved.

For more information or permission contact:
boehmduane@gmail.com

This book is a work of fiction. References to real people, events, establishments, organizations, or locales are intended only to provide a sense of authenticity and are used fictitiously. All other characters, and all incidents and dialogue are drawn from the author's imagination and not to be construed as real.

ISBN: 9781542312066

Other Books by Duane Boehm

In Just One Moment
Gideon Johann: A Gideon Johann Western Prequel
Last Stand: A Gideon Johann Western Book 1
Last Chance: A Gideon Johann Western Book 2
Last Hope: A Gideon Johann Western Book 3
Last Ride: A Gideon Johann Western Book 4
Last Breath: A Gideon Johann Western Book 5
Last Journey: A Gideon Johann Western Book 6
Wayward Brother: A Gideon Johann Western Book 8
Where The Wild Horses Roam: Wild Horse Westerns Book 1
Spirit Of The Wild Horse: Wild Horse Westerns Book 2
Wild Horse On The Run: Wild Horse Westerns Book 3
What It All Comes Down To
Hand Of Fate: The Hand Of Westerns Book 1
Hand Of The Father: The Hand Of Westerns Book 2
Trail To Yesterday
Sun Over The Mountains
Wanted: A Collection of Western Stories (7 authors)
Wanted II: A Collection of Western Stories (7 authors)

Dedicated to Josh Kirby

Chapter 1

Fancy Broderick covered her mouth in surprise when Andrew Moss walked into the Pearl West Saloon just before closing time. The whore had been sweet on him back in the day. They had even talked of marriage and getting her out of the trade, but that was before laudanum became his real one true love. He had looked like death warmed over the last time she had seen him, but there he stood alive and kicking. That wasn't to say that he still didn't look like hell. He was nothing but skin and bones and he appeared a good fifteen years older than his forty years. His eyes were glazed and he looked as if he were in a stupor as he spied her. Andrew smiled as he shuffled over to Fancy.

"Fancy meeting you here," Andrew said, grinning proudly at his pun. "What have you been up to lately?"

"Buy me a drink and we can sit and talk," Fancy said.

"Two glasses of whiskey, Jimmy," Andrew called out to the bartender.

The big bartender, who doubled as the saloon's enforcer, eyed Andrew warily. Trouble and Andrew Moss went together like ducks and water in his opinion. He poured two glasses of whiskey and shoved them across the bar. Fancy retrieved the drinks and walked to a table away from the other patrons.

"I guess you found us," Fancy said as she and Andrew sat down at the table.

"Yeah, word about Cyrus's whereabouts gets around."

Cyrus Capello owned the Pearl West and had a reputation for his ruthlessness. Smart enough to be discreet in his crimes, he would pack up his saloon and move to a new town when the law started closing in on him. The sheriffs and marshals were always so relieved to get Cyrus out of their hair that they would drop their investigations of him to ensure his departure.

"You are high," Fancy said.

Andrew chuckled. "I'm always high."

Fancy gazed into Andrew's eyes. If she focused only on the twinkle they still possessed, she could allow herself to get a little misty for him. Andrew had been a fine man before falling from his horse and breaking his arm. After that, the laudanum washed away whatever admirable traits he once possessed. Still, all in all, he had treated her better than just about any man had that she could remember.

"So what brings you to town?"

Lowering his head, Andrew whispered, "I'm about out of money. I saw Cyrus kill Dog Ear Calloway. He's going to pay me to keep my mouth shut or else."

Looking around before leaning forward, Fancy raised her eyebrows and whispered, "Are you crazy? Cyrus or Jimmy will kill you so fast that you won't even know you died. Don't do it. You know full well that Cyrus is not a man to be trifled with."

"I've known Cyrus since we were both slop boys in the saloons of Saint Louie. I smashed a whiskey bottle upside the head of a saloonkeeper that was going to do some cutting on Cyrus. We headed out west together after that. He wouldn't hurt me. We go too far back."

"You know that the only thing in this whole world that Cyrus cares about is his money," Fancy said.

Andrew took a sip of whiskey, savoring the liquor before swallowing. "I still don't think he'd do me harm, and besides, I hear that this Sheriff Johann is a lot smarter than most of these fools posing as sheriffs. Johann might get suspicious if I turned up dead."

"Gideon will never find you if you turn up dead. You know better than that. Cyrus and Jimmy know how to make a body disappear. The sheriff isn't anybody's fool, that's for sure, and he's honest, but Cyrus knows his way around the block, too. Sheriff Johann already turned Deputy Ford loose on Cyrus after Cyrus hired an arsonist to burn down the saloon of the deputy's wife. Finnie beat the daylights out of Cyrus and then cut a chunk of skin out of his eyebrow. Don't dare stare at it if you talk to Cyrus. It makes him mad," Fancy said and then took a big gulp of whiskey to calm herself. From the expression on Andrew's face, she could see that she was losing the battle.

As Andrew tipped up the glass to his lips, he drained the remainder of his drink. He smiled at Fancy with the grin he had used to steal her heart. "We had us some pretty good times back in the day. I thought you were going to make an honest man out of me. What happened?"

"You know what happened. You loved that damn laudanum more than you ever did me. We could have made a nice life for ourselves if you had wanted it bad enough," Fancy said as she searched Andrew's face for any sign of regret for the way things stood between them.

"After I go talk to Cyrus, we may go have us some loving for old time's sake," Andrew said as he stood.

Fancy reached over and grabbed Andrew's hand. "Andrew, I'm begging you not to do it."

Looking towards the bar, Andrew hollered, "Hey, Jimmy, I need to talk to Cyrus right now."

Jimmy scurried to the back of the saloon and quickly returned, motioning for Andrew with his finger. Andrew gave Fancy one last smile before following the big bartender into the back.

Fancy watched Andrew walk away, sure that she was seeing him alive for the last time. Her body suddenly seemed so heavy and sluggish that she had to force herself to stand. Life as a whore aged a girl, and at that moment, she felt plenty old. She walked to the far end of the bar where her line of sight through the entrance to the back part of the saloon let her see the door to Cyrus's office. His door was shut. She stared at it trying to will Andrew to walk back out to her. Needing to calm herself, she poured another glass of whiskey and took a big gulp. The passing minutes seemed an eternity and she swore that the pendulum on the clock behind the bar slowed its swing as she listened to its tick-tock. Finally, Jimmy opened the door, walking out trying to dab blood off his shirt. Giving up, he draped the towel over the spot.

"All right, everybody, it's closing time. Come back to see us tomorrow," Jimmy yelled and started shooing the cowboys out of the saloon. "You whores get on up to your rooms."

Fancy had no intention of going anywhere. Her willpower fought an epic battle with her stomach to keep from puking all over the bar. She wanted to cry, but instead pursed her lips tightly together and stared at the liquor bottles across the bar to avoid betraying any emotion. The last thing that she needed was for Cyrus to think she had feelings for Andrew.

Cyrus walked out of his office and over to the bar. "Jimmy says that you were talking to Andrew. Did you have any part of this?" he asked coldly.

"I told the damn fool not to try it, but he wouldn't listen. He thought you were his friend and would give him the money," Fancy answered.

"Money is my friend. Don't you ever forget that and make sure you keep your mouth shut," Cyrus warned.

"I always do, don't I?"

Ignoring her, Cyrus walked back to his office and dragged Andrew out into the hall. Andrew's throat had been slit from ear to ear so deeply that his head flopped about as if it might fall off the body. "Jimmy, go find his horse and bring it around back," Cyrus instructed.

Fancy began gagging, her self-control all gone. She turned her head and vomited onto the floor until her stomach had emptied. Sucking in a breath of air before speaking, she looked at Cyrus and said, "Why didn't you just go ahead and cut his head off while you were at it."

"Clean up your mess and then start cleaning up this one. And watch your damn mouth," Cyrus yelled before dragging the body away and into the alley.

Jimmy and Cyrus hoisted Andrew across his saddle. As Jimmy mounted his own horse, Cyrus handed him a shovel.

"Make sure you ride a long ways out of town and bury that idiot where nobody will find him," Cyrus ordered.

"It's going to be kind of hard to see in the dark," Jimmy protested. "I don't know my way around here that well."

"Quit your complaining. You have enough moonlight to see. Just get the damn job done right unless you want to be hanged beside me," Cyrus said before turning and entering the back door of the saloon.

Chapter 2

Arising before anyone else in the Pearl West, Fancy walked down the stairs and into the back of the saloon to make some coffee. She'd barely slept during the night. Between fits of crying over the murder of Andrew, and the fact that her twat burned and itched like crazy, sleep had been hard to come by. Every time that Stubby Blake had a poke with her, she ended up ready to claw herself raw. She could never get it through Cyrus's greedy head that the five dollars that they made off Stubby always put her out of work for a couple of days and cost them in the long run. Cyrus lived by the theory that a bird in the hand is worth two in the bush.

Doc Abram wasn't scheduled to do his weekly check of the saloon girls until Wednesday and there was no way that Fancy could wait until then. She would have to listen to Cyrus bitch about her making a visit to the doctor, but she didn't care. After sitting down at the table, she sipped her coffee and worried whether Andrew had been buried deep enough that the coyotes and wolves wouldn't be gnawing on his bones.

By the time that she'd drained the last sip from her cup, Fancy figured the doctor's office would be open. She still hadn't seen another soul from the Pearl West that morning and that suited her just fine. Slipping out the back door, she caught sight of the dried pool of blood that had formed after Andrew had been thrown across his horse's saddle. Her stomach started coming up into her throat and she skedaddled down the alley.

Fancy found Doc sitting at his desk drinking coffee and reading the paper. Like most everyone else in Last Stand, she had developed a deep affection for the lovable old curmudgeon. Unlike most doctors she had dealt with in the past, Doc Abram treated her and the other whores just as if they were respectable citizens of the town with his typical grousing and compassion.

Looking up over the paper, Doc asked, "Fancy, what brings you in to see me?"

"Doc, my money-maker is itching so bad that I want to take a scrub brush to it. You need to fix whatever ails Stubby Blake so that you don't have to fix me all the time," Fancy said as shucked garments and hopped up onto the table without a trace of embarrassment.

"Stubby never comes in here. You need to have Cyrus put an end to Stubby being your customer," Doc said as he retrieved a bottle of vinegar from the shelf.

"Lot of luck I'll have with that. Cyrus won't ever leave money on the table."

Grabbing a large syringe, the doctor filled it with vinegar. He began flushing out the young woman's vagina until the acidic smell of the liquid drowned out the fishy odor that permeated the room. As he worked, Doc asked, "So how is life at the Pearl West?"

Fancy looked away from Doc's gaze for the first time that morning as if the question caused her more distress than the procedure going on between her legs. "It's a living and I've worked for worse than Cyrus though that's not saying much."

"Did you ever think about getting out of the trade?"

Making a small chortle, Fancy said, "And do what? I'm not fit for much else. I had a man want to marry me once, but I lost out to his love for laudanum. His name was Andrew Moss. That was my one chance."

"What happened to him?" Doc inquired.

"Funny you should ask. He showed up last night and Cyrus and Jimmy slit his throat. There's blood all over the alley," Fancy blurted out.

Doc suddenly stopped squeezing the syringe midway through the flush. His eyebrows raised and his eyes grew large. "What?" he asked.

"Nothing, I was just talking. Forget I ever said anything," she said, rushing her words.

"Fancy, if you know of a murder last night, you need to tell the sheriff."

"And if Cyrus finds out I did that, I'd be as dead as Andrew, and the sheriff couldn't do one thing about it," Fancy said, her voice rising with each word.

"I'd think that you'd want justice for a man that you cared about."

"Justice won't bring him back and will likely get me killed. Even if Cyrus did go to jail, I'd be out of a job."

"Let me walk across the street and get Gideon. He'll protect you."

Pursing her lips and scowling, her voice sounded shrill and hostile. "If you walk out of here, I'll be back in the saloon by the time you return. My twat can rot off in the meantime."

The doctor didn't speak, but returned to his work. After he had treated her with the vinegar to his satisfaction, he put an ointment into the syringe and administered it. He handed her the syringe, a bottle of vinegar, and the jar of ointment. "Repeat what I've done twice a day. No men for two days."

"Thank you, Doc," Fancy said. The anger had left her and she sounded meek and harmless.

"Fancy, I have to tell Gideon to go look in the alley," Doc said.

"Do what you have to do, but you'll get no cooperation from me. I know that sheriff would try to do right by me, but Cyrus is a force to be reckoned with. He'd find a way to kill me."

"I think you underestimate Gideon. Go on and get back to the saloon. Maybe nobody has missed you," Doc said before turning to scrub his hands.

After Fancy had gone, Doc methodically dried his hands before shuffling across the street and into the jail. Sheriff Gideon Johann sat at his desk sipping coffee while Deputy Finnie Ford sat across from him doing the same. Both men were used to the doctor coming over for morning coffee and barely glanced his way.

"This is just what I needed," Finnie said in his heavy Irish brogue as he looked towards the doctor. "Gideon is in an ill mood and you always are. What's a poor Irishman to do? There's certainly no one here to appreciate my fine sense of humor."

Doc poured himself a cup of coffee and sat down beside Finnie before saying anything. "What you and Gideon need to do is take a walk into the alley behind the Pearl West. Rumor has it that you'll find a lot of blood," he said before taking a sip of coffee and watching the two men's reactions as both sat upright in their chairs.

"What are you talking about?" Gideon asked as he habitually started rubbing the scar on his cheekbone.

"Fancy came for a visit and let slip that an old beau of hers showed up and Cyrus and Jimmy killed him last night. His name is Andrew Moss. She said there's a lot of blood in the alley," Doc said.

"I can't keep all those whores straight. Which one is Fancy?" Gideon asked.

"The redhead with the green eyes. She told me in no uncertain terms that she would not cooperate with you. She fears Cyrus will kill her, too," Doc replied.

"I guess we better figure out if we have a murder on our hands before we worry about getting her to talk. I knew there was a reason I didn't want to get out of bed this morning. Cyrus was bound to cause us trouble again one of these days," Gideon said in a dour voice.

Standing, Finnie said, "It's kind of like the cowboy that swore off visiting the whorehouse. Best intentions go out the door when you get that itch that needs scratching."

Gideon looked at Finnie and just shook his head as he ran his hand through his mop of hair before putting on his hat.

"You two haven't earned your pay since you calmed things down between the sheepherders and the ranchers. Quit your bellyaching and go do your job," Doc said as he headed towards the door.

"If you're so worried about the taxpayer's money, you should start paying for the coffee you mooch off us most mornings," Gideon said just before Doc walked out of the jail.

"Look at the bright side, maybe we'll be able to put Cyrus away and not have to deal with him anymore," Finnie said.

"I was just thinking that same thing. I'm feeling better already. Let's take a walk to the alley and see if Fancy knows what she's talking about," Gideon said.

The two law officers walked down the street before crossing over and heading to the alley behind the saloon. Both men spied the remnants of the pool of blood several steps before reaching the spot. As Finnie squatted down for a closer look, Gideon walked on up the alleyway looking for more blood.

"They had to have thrown him over a horse and he bled out as he was led away. There's a trail of blood a child could follow," Gideon said.

"I'm guessing that they slit his throat for there to be this much blood or maybe a stab to the heart, but I doubt that," Finnie remarked.

Gideon spotted the shovel leaning up against the saloon with fresh dirt still encrusted on the metal. "Looks like they buried him," he said as he grabbed the shovel. "Go to the livery stable and get your horse, an extra mount, and a tarp. Meet me at the jail."

By the time Finnie returned with the horses, Gideon already sat atop his horse waiting. He handed the shovel to his deputy. "Stick it in the spare horse's scabbard," he said and grinned. "It's not good for my image to be riding around holding a shovel."

"Being Gideon Johann is not good for your image either," Finnie said as he mounted his horse.

Spring weather had finally chased away the last vestige of winter and the warm sun made for pleasant riding. Just being away from the jail improved Gideon's mood to the point that he became unusually loquacious. The change in mood caused Finnie to glance over at his friend as if he were riding with an impostor.

For the first mile, tracking the blood required little attention. After that, the blood trail became sparser until the two men had to dismount and walk to spot the droplets. They walked for another mile before seeing where two horses had left the road and headed off into the brush. Walking a good hundred yards, the terrain changed to grassland where they found the grave.

Holding out the shovel, Gideon said, "Well, start digging and let's see what we find."

"What?" Finnie said with exasperation. "Do I look like a Scotsman to you? The Scottish love to run around in their skirts and rob graves. That's how they get so rich. We Irish have a little more pride in our character."

With his arm straight out and the shovel handle right in front of Finnie's face, Gideon said, "Last time I checked, we were still in the United States. I don't care about your disdain for the Scots. You work for me so dig. I'll spell you if you get tired."

Finnie grabbed the shovel and began mumbling while Gideon sat down in the grass, tilting his hat back so the sun hit his face.

"Sure is a beautiful day," Gideon said.

"It might get a lot more beautiful if I lay this shovel upside a certain sheriff's head and add a second body to this here grave," Finnie groused.

"Look who's in an ill mood now. You should enjoy being out in nature more."

By the time Finnie had dug down the three feet to the body, the armpits of his shirt were soaked in sweat and he continuously mopped his brow with his sleeve. "Are you going to help me drag the body out or do I have to do that myself too?"

"I can do that," Gideon said as he arose to his feet.

Each man grabbed a leg of the deceased man and began pulling him out of the hole. As Andrew Moss's shoulders cleared the grave, his head flopped grotesquely backwards as if it were trying to roll back into the grave.

"Good God, they damn near cut off that poor man's head. No wonder there was blood everywhere," Finnie lamented as he turned his back to the body.

"And don't think that Cyrus wouldn't love to do the same to me and you," Gideon said as he rolled Andrew over to get most of the dirt off the body.

"Gideon, we have to put that dago away. He's a danger to our town."

"You won't get any argument from me," Gideon said as he rifled through the pockets of the dead man. "He doesn't have any papers on him. We'll have to pretend like we don't know who he is or Cyrus will figure out that the whore talked."

"Her name is Fancy Broderick."

"Yes, you're right. I shouldn't just call her the whore. Let's get the body wrapped up and across the saddle. We need to get back to town."

After Gideon and Finnie secured the body across the saddle, they walked the horses back to the road and mounted up.

"So what's your plan?" Finnie asked.

"I don't think we'll do anything for now besides talk to District Attorney Kile. The judge was just here last week and it'll be a good month before he returns. There's no need to endanger Fancy Broderick yet. I fear that even if we locked Cyrus and Jimmy up that something would happen to her. She'll be the key to getting a conviction and we'll have to wear her down when the time is right. We'll just let Cyrus and Jimmy stew on this and wonder what we're up to."

"I'd pull the lever for the pleasure of watching Cyrus Capello swing," Finnie said before spitting on the ground.

As the lawmen reached the side street next to the Pearl West, they turned down it and then rode into the alley behind the saloon. Jimmy was busy stacking empty whiskey barrels as they approached. Even though the bartender could make almost two of the sheriff, Gideon watched Jimmy cower a little. On a previous occasion, Gideon had laid his Colt upside the thug's head and made a lasting impression upon the bartender.

Holding out the shovel, Gideon said, "Thanks for the use of your shovel. You wouldn't know anything about this here body, would you? We followed the blood from this alley to find him.

Gideon could see the color literally drain from Jimmy's face as the bartender retreated a step with the shovel clutched in his hand.

"Uh, uh, no, sir, I don't know a thing about it. Maybe a couple of our patrons had a fight back here," Jimmy said.

"Well, come over here and have a peek at him. I need to see if anybody knows who he is," Gideon said.

Jimmy looked down the alley as if he were contemplating his options before leaning the shovel against the side of the building. He walked slowly towards the body and struggled to burrow through the tarp to find Andrew's head. Grabbing the hair, he tilted the head up and gave it a good look. "I don't believe I've ever seen him before, but I don't make a habit of noticing my customers."

"Surely you could tell me some of the regulars that were in last night," Gideon said.

"The nights all run together, and besides, I tend to look at their money and not their face."

"Just checking," Gideon said as he heeled Buck into moving on down the alley.

As Jimmy ran into the saloon, he screamed for Cyrus.

Cyrus came running out of his office. "What in the hell is going on out here?" he shouted.

"That damn sheriff and his deputy already found the body," Jimmy stammered.

"Damn it. What did you do, put up a sign advertising an unmarked grave?" Cyrus yelled.

"They followed the blood trail from the alley," Jimmy replied sheepishly.

"I told you to clean up all the mess," Cyrus roared. The color rose up in his face and his eyes bulged to the point that a stroke appeared imminent.

"I never thought about the alley and it was too dark to see good."

"What in the hell was that sheriff doing looking in the alley in the first place? Fancy," Cyrus bellowed.

Fancy emerged from the room in the back of the saloon. "What is it, Cyrus?"

"Have you been talking to anyone?" Cyrus asked.

"All the other whores are still asleep. Jimmy is the only person I've seen all morning," Fancy lied.

"Johann has already found Andrew's body. I should have never moved to this town. That sheriff is too smart for his own good."

Realizing that she would need an excuse for the medicine in her room and the fact that she couldn't do tricks for a couple of days, Fancy said, "Stubby Blake has got me itching bad again. I need to go see Doc."

"Very well. Just keep your mouth shut. I don't know why you let Stubby put his pecker in you. He puts your money-maker out of business every time he does."

Biting her lip, Fancy looked at Cyrus with a look that could kill.

Chapter 3

Waking up the morning after finding the body of Andrew Moss, Gideon arose relieved that it was Saturday and he had no plans of going to town. After leaving the body with the undertaker the previous day, he had met with the district attorney, given an interview with the newspaper editor where he feigned ignorance to the identity of the body, and then suffered through what felt like an interrogation by every citizen of Last Stand as he walked the town. He loved Last Stand, but he sometimes wondered if its townsfolk were the nosiest citizenry in the whole of Colorado.

The smell of frying bacon and eggs lured Gideon into the kitchen where his wife, Abby, stood at the stove cooking. She gave him a smile and a kiss as he walked up to greet her. His stepdaughter, Winnie, and his young son, Chance, sat at the table impatiently waiting for their breakfasts. Winnie talked in her usual rapid-fire way to Chance, explaining that the family planned to go to Joann and Zack's place for a big feast.

Joann was Gideon and Abby's daughter, born out of wedlock after Gideon had left for the war, and raised by Abby's aunt and uncle in the Wyoming Territory. Abby had married and divorced Winnie's father in the ensuing years before marrying Gideon and having Chance. The get-together was significant in that it would be the first time that Joann had chosen to host company after the death of her and Zack's infant the previous year. The young woman had been inconsolable after Tess's death and had at one point returned to Wyoming to live with the parents that had raised her. Since returning to Last Stand, she had gradually begun to act more like her old self again.

As Abby forked bacon onto a plate, she looked over at her daughter. "You better stay out of the swimming hole today. The weather is not near warm enough for swimming, and if you think you're going to pull that trick on me twice, you will be sadly embarrassed in front of a lot of our friends."

Grinning sheepishly, Winnie said, "We did it for a good cause last time."

"So you say," Abby said as she and Gideon brought the food to the table.

After the family scarfed down their breakfasts as if they hadn't eaten in a week, Abby began the laborious task of heating water for everyone to take baths. By the time all of the baths were completed and the children's hair combed to their mother's satisfaction, the family needed to leave. Gideon had the buckboard wagon already hitched and hastily lifted the children aboard. Abby, elated that Joann showed signs of moving past the death of Tess, led Winnie and Chance in singing songs the entire trip.

By the time Gideon and his family pulled into the yard, Finnie, along with his wife, Mary, and son, Sam, had arrived with Doc in the doctor's buggy. The men were sitting out on the front porch and Gideon sat down with them. Abby joined Mary and Joann in the kitchen to help with preparing the meal while Winnie insisted on taking Sam from Finnie to rock the baby inside the cabin.

"So how has Joann been?" Gideon asked Zack.

Zack smiled at his father-in-law's directness. He appreciated that he never had to guess what Gideon thought about a subject. "Pretty darn good. She gets better by the week. She still has some bad days, but she comes out of it quickly and without prodding from me. Life is good again."

"You did a fine job with helping her. I'm proud of you," Gideon said.

Not sure what to say, Zack looked down at his feet and appeared as awkward as when Gideon had first brought the young man to town.

Never one to tolerate silence, Finnie said, "You should feel honored. I've saved Gideon's life before and barely got an acknowledgement from him."

"That's because you pat yourself on the back enough for five men."

"Ain't that the truth," Doc chimed in.

"I'm about as wanted as the chunky girl in the whorehouse," Finnie remarked.

"Here comes Ethan and company," Gideon said, nodding his head towards the driveway.

The buckboard pulled up into the yard and Ethan helped down his wife, Sarah, before lifting out Sylvia, the four-year-old orphan the family had taken into their home the previous fall after the rest of her family had perished in a house fire. Benjamin, the couples' son, hopped out of the wagon and began scanning the yard in search of Winnie.

Ethan Oakes had been Gideon's best friend since they started school together. Their bond had survived years of no interaction and had somehow come through it unscathed. Since Gideon's return to Last Stand, Sarah had become one of Gideon's confidants and he loved her like the sister he never had.

As Sarah walked up onto the porch, she sported a devilish grin. "Looks like all of you have found your true calling."

Pushing his hat back off his forehead, Gideon said, "You best get inside and find yours. We're hungry."

"Gideon Johann, you're either a very brave man today or have lost your mind. I'd watch every bite of my food if I were you," Sarah said before leading Sylvia into the cabin.

After sitting down beside Gideon, Ethan looked over at Zack and asked, "Have you got your alfalfa sowed yet?"

"Finished yesterday," Zack answered.

"Glad to hear it. Are you going to be able to start helping me?" Ethan inquired.

"I should be able to come over Monday."

As Ethan looked around to make sure no women were in hearing range, he said, "Thank goodness. Fuzzy Clark is about as useless as tits on a boar hog. I can use you."

The men continued talking out on the porch until Abby summoned them for the meal. As the adults maneuvered to get seated at a table not nearly large enough for the number of people attempting to sit at it, Joann stood waiting patiently. Zack looked up from his seat, surprised that his wife had not joined him.

Once the chairs stopped scooting on the floor and everybody got situated, Joann said, "Zack and I want to thank everyone for coming. I guess we'll call this a spring celebration for lack of anything better. Everything is greening up, leafing out, and starting anew. I feel like that's what I'm doing too, at least on most days. What I really want to do is thank each and every one of you for being there for me when I wasn't at my best. I know that I was a mess, and I'm sure some of you thought that you were wasting your time and your breath on me, but you all made a difference. I know you are all hungry, but I just want to say that I love all of you." She began fanning herself and her eyes rimmed with tears.

An embarrassed silence followed so Sarah began clapping to end the awkwardness and the others followed suit. Joann blushed and scurried to her seat. In an attempt to ward of his stomach from making loud growling sounds, Ethan quickly began saying the blessing.

The group fell into easy conversation on subjects as varied as the weather to the price of cattle. As they talked, they gorged themselves on beefsteaks, potatoes, and corn topped off with an apple cobbler. By the time the meal was finished, the men were leaning back in their chairs, patting their bellies, and complaining about how much food they had eaten.

"All the men outside right now," Joann ordered. "We can't gossip proper around the male persuasion."

Abby stood and began gathering plates. "Winnie, take Chance outside to play and keep a close eye on him."

"But Momma, I wanted to play with Sylvia and Benjamin," Winnie whined.

"You can do both. Either take him with you or stay in here and wash dishes," Abby threatened.

Winnie held out her hand to her brother and led him out the door with Benjamin and Sylvia following behind them. The men arose from their seats and walked out onto the porch. Ethan and Gideon began loading their pipes with tobacco and Finnie pulled a stogie from his pocket, biting off the cap and lighting the cigar.

After taking his first puff and blowing a plume of smoke into the air, Finnie asked, "Doc, have you had any luck with finding a doctor to help you?"

"Not a one. I just can't figure out the problem. Nobody apparently wants to get their start in a small town here in the west. Those grandkids of mine are going to be up and grown by the time I see them again," Doc complained.

Doc had conceived a son with the daughter of a prominent banker from Boston while he attended medical school. The girl's family used their influence to keep the future doctor from ever seeing the child, and Doc eventually gave up on being a part of his son's life so he moved to Last Stand. The son, named John, had visited his father for the first time a couple of years ago after the death of his mother. He had then brought his whole family out west the previous summer. After meeting his grandchildren, Doc had been smitten and longed to spend more time with the family.

"You need to talk John into bringing the family out for a visit again this summer," Finnie said.

"That's easier said than done. A banker has a lot of responsibilities. John and Kate have both written me, wanting me to retire and move in with them. I've been thinking seriously about it even though I'm a bit irritated that I haven't received a letter from them recently."

The four other men all exchanged glances with one another and Finnie looked visibly shaken.

"You can't do that," Finnie demanded.

Looking agitated, Doc asked, "And why not?"

"First off, you can't up and leave the town without a doctor, and second, who would I have to argue with if you weren't here? When we named Sam after you, I thought you'd be around to see him grow up," Finnie said in a voice that sounded like a jilted lover pleading for one more chance.

Doc studied Finnie for a moment. Sometimes he still marveled at the bond he had developed with the little, loud Irishman. The two men had so little in common and they certainly never had very deep conversations, but something about Finnie made the doctor feel good to be in the Irishman's company. "Finnie, I'm old. I seriously doubt I will still be living by the time that Sam is a young man. I'd like to spend some time with the grandkids before I die."

"Well, I don't like this talk," Finnie said before pretending to concentrate on smoking his cigar.

"So how is Abby doing on building your ranching empire?" Ethan asked Gideon.

"I guess that depends on how good those young bulls you sold her turn out to be. Her and String are excited about all their plans. I try to stay out of it as much as possible. That's her baby. Next year's calves will show us if those two know what they are doing," Gideon replied.

"Those bulls will produce. I'm sure of that. I should have kept that dark one for myself, but Abby can be persuasive," Ethan said and smiled.

"You can call it persuasive, but as her husband, I would say it's more like a dog with a bone that you give in to because you're tired of all the growling," Gideon said with a chuckle.

"All of you married men are big talkers as long as your wives are out of hearing range," Doc remarked.

"Well, at least we were brave enough to climb onto that horse and ride," Finnie said.

Playing dumb, Doc asked, "What's a horse got to do with marriage?"

"No wonder nobody will come work for you," Finnie said before taking a puff on his stogie and blowing the smoke into the air in a big show.

Zack watched the four children running around playing tag and thought about his dead daughter and how Tess would never know the joy of running around giggling as if she hadn't a care in the world. He could feel his spirit sagging, and to get Tess off his mind, he looked at Ethan and asked, "So how is Sylvia doing?"

"You know, she's doing pretty well. She still goes to bed with us, but we're able to carry her to her own bed after she falls asleep, and she now makes it through the night without any nightmares. I know she still misses her parents and brother, but she certainly is part of our family now. Benjamin has been so good and patient with her. I can't imagine not having her with us," Ethan said proudly.

"That fire was certainly a tragedy, but at least some good came of it. We can thank Finnie for that," Doc said.

Finnie would always get embarrassed at the mention of his rescue of the child and turn red. "It wasn't anything that any one of us wouldn't have done. I was just unlucky enough to be the first one there," he said before feigning a yawn.

For the rest of the afternoon, the men sat on the porch talking and the women stayed inside doing the same. The children finally tired of skipping rocks across the swimming hole and trudged back to the cabin.

"You two look exhausted. Go see if your momma is ready to go home," Gideon said to Winnie and Chance as the children walked up onto the porch.

After everyone got all of their goodbyes out of the way, all of the guests departed at the same time. Zack and Joann stood on the porch waving until the wagons disappeared out of sight.

On the ride home, Winnie stood up in the back of the buckboard and placed her hands on her mother's shoulder. "Do you know what Sylvia said today?" she asked.

"No, what did Sylvia say?" Abby asked.

"She said that one of these days that she is going to go find Heaven."

"Oh, honey, Sylvia is too young to understand about death and Heaven. She still misses her parents and brother and thinks she can go visit them someday. Just try to be understanding."

"Oh, we were. Benjamin and I both told her that we hoped we all got to go there eventually," Winnie said.

Chapter 4

Gideon walked into the jail Monday morning to find Finnie sitting across from the desk sipping coffee with a scowl on his face that made the sheriff think his deputy looked like an angry, old leprechaun.

"Good God, what's wrong with you?" Gideon asked.

"All that nonsense about Doc retiring and moving to Boston has put a burr under my saddle," Finnie complained.

"Last time I checked, you weren't married to Doc. He's devoted his life to this place and if he wants to spend the rest of his time here on earth with his family, he's certainly earned the right," Gideon reasoned as he poured himself a cup of coffee.

"This town would be in a fix without him. And I thought all of us made a pretty good family for him."

"We do, but Doc never got to raise John. Think how you would feel about never getting to see Sam. He's got a taste of the joy of those grandkids of his and he wants more of it."

"He can come and get Sam anytime that he wants," Finnie said defensively.

Shaking his head, Gideon dropped into his chair. "When push comes to shove, I don't think he'll do it anyways so quit your worrying," he said and tossed his hat onto the desk.

"So what are we going to do for fun today?"

"Speaking of burrs under the saddle, I'm going to go rile Cyrus up this morning."

"Do you want me to come with you?"

"Nah, you know how I feel about that. I don't want him to ever think it takes the two of us to handle his sorry ass."

The two men drank the rest of their coffee in silence. Gideon stood up, deciding to make a walk of the town. Finnie's mood put a damper on his own spirit and he wanted to get away from it before he got as depressed as the Irishman.

By the time Gideon had walked the town, and talked to several merchants, Jimmy stood out in front of the Pearl West sweeping the boardwalk. Gideon walked past the bartender and into the saloon without so much as a greeting. Cyrus sat drinking coffee at one of the tables. The saloonkeeper looked hungover. His eyes were bloodshot and his face puffy. The smell of whiskey still clung to him like an empty liquor bottle. In an attempt to agitate Cyrus, Gideon made a point to stare at the eyebrow that Finnie had sliced a piece of hide out of its arch. The saloon owner used black boot polish to cover up the scarred, bare skin. The attempt to hide the missing hair looked ridiculous and drew more attention to it than if Cyrus had left the eyebrow alone, especially when he would rub his face and smear the polish across his forehead.

Gideon sat down at the table. "You look like hell."

"Easy access to the product is one of the downsides of owning a saloon," Cyrus said, his voice hoarse and croaky.

"What do you know about the man that was murdered here?" Gideon asked as he tapped his finger on the table.

"It didn't happen in here, and if it happened in the alley, I don't know a thing about it. Since nobody knows his name, and I never saw the body, I can't even say if he was in here or not."

"I figured as much. You and Jimmy seem to have a poor memory," Gideon said, never taking his eye off Cyrus's eyebrow.

Cyrus acted as if his forehead itched and used his hand to cover the disfigurement as he scratched. "I'm afraid I'm of no assistance to you. Things like murders are bad for business. I wouldn't be no party to such a thing," he said with a slight touch of mockery.

"Cyrus, you picked the wrong town to pull your shenanigans in. If you stay around here, I'll eventually put you away for your crimes. In the meantime, you better keep your nose clean or I'm going to turn Finnie loose on that other eyebrow," Gideon said as he stood.

"Or maybe you picked the wrong town in which to be sheriff. You shouldn't threaten the fine citizenry of Last Stand without provocation. It makes you look like a thug instead of the law. And as for your deputy, I won't be pulling a knife on him the next time. He'll never get close enough to me to take away a gun like he did with my knife. I'll use it to blow off his head," Cyrus said in a voice so full of venom that a lesser man than the sheriff might have been scared, but Gideon had learned long ago to never fear just talk.

Walking out of the saloon, Gideon sucked in a breath of air and puffed out his cheeks as he exhaled loudly. Cyrus Capello got under his skin, and he didn't like letting someone as worthless as the saloon owner do that. It just galled him that he knew Cyrus had committed the murder along with other crimes, but could never be even brought to trial for lack of evidence.

Gideon was in no mood to sit in the jail or be around Finnie's dour mood. He hurried past his office and into the alley behind the Last Chance Last Stand Saloon. Finnie's wife, Mary, owned the establishment. She served as the sheriff's sounding board when he needed someone in town to talk to that would give him the unvarnished truth whether he wanted to hear it or not. He entered through the back door and was surprised to find Mary holding Sam with one arm and writing with her other hand.

"Mrs. Penny felt ill this morning and I had to make an order today so I had no choice but to bring Sam with me," Mary explained.

"You should have made Finnie stay home with the baby. He's about useless today anyway, but he probably would have had the baby crying the whole time," Gideon said as he sat down at the table.

"You're telling me. Doc has got him all torn up. I told him Doc will never leave when it's all said and done."

"I told him the same thing, though I wouldn't blame Doc if he did."

"You didn't come here to complain about my husband. What's going on?"

"I went to see Cyrus about the murder. That greasy Italian makes my skin crawl. I guess I'm starting to think that he's smarter than me and I'll never put him away."

"Finnie told me that Fancy can tie him to the murder."

"That's what Doc says. I'm afraid she'll end up dead if I try to talk to her before the judge gets here. She's scared."

"Gideon, Cyrus Capello is not smarter than you. You'll eventually bring him down. If not this time, sometime soon. Men like him always let greed get the better part of their judgement eventually."

"You think so?" Gideon asked doubtfully.

Reaching over and patting Gideon's hand, Mary said, "I don't know why you always doubt yourself. I'd put you and that husband of mine up against anyone and never have a concern."

"Let me know if you learn of anybody that was in the Pearl West that night. It wouldn't hurt to have some collaboration that Andrew Moss was in there before he died."

"I'll do it."

Smiling, Gideon said, "Saturday proved to be a good day, didn't it?"

"Yes, it did. Joann seemed darn near her old self. She even rocked Sam and seemed at peace with herself when she did. You're liable to get another chance at being a grandpa again one of these days."

"I sure hope so. I'll never stop thinking about Tess though."

"And you shouldn't, but it's time that you just remember the joy she brought to your family and not the sadness," Mary said as she passed Sam to Gideon. "Hold him, I got work to do."

Chapter 5

Glancing up to see the time on clock in the jail, Finnie decided to make a walk of Last Stand. He made it his habit to try to check out the passengers arriving by stagecoach each scheduled trip. Part of his reasoning was to be on the lookout for possible criminals arriving in town and the other was that he was just plain nosey. He loved to beat Doc to the punch with new gossip.

As Finnie walked the town, he stopped to talk to townsfolk and merchants to kill time. As the stagecoach came into view down the street, he sauntered to the bench in front of the arrival station and took a seat. The stage pulled up and Finnie did a double take as the first passenger stepping out was Doc's son, John Hamilton. John helped his wife, Kate, down before their three children departed.

Finnie stood and walked over to the stage. "John, what a surprise. Does Doc know that you were coming?"

John turned and spotted the deputy for the first time. "Finnie, good to see you," he said as he shook hands. "No, this is a surprise. We all were dying to come back out here so here we are."

"I guess that's why he hasn't received a letter from you lately. He was complaining about that the other day."

Kate stepped up and gave Finnie a peck on the cheek. "How is that baby doing?" she asked.

"Sam is growing like a weed. He'll be a year old before you know it. He's starting to walk some and talk a little. Mary will be so glad to see you."

"I can't wait to see them. We plan to take your doctor back to Boston with us. I won't take no for an answer," Kate said.

Finnie tried to hide his displeasure with Kate's statement, but failed miserably. The notion that Doc could leave Last Stand gave him the same pangs he had experienced the first time a girl had broken his heart. "I don't know what this town would do without him and he can't find another doctor to come here. This may be selfish, but I sure hope he stays."

Seeming to grow in stature as she straightened her posture, Kate said, "Doc has devoted his whole life to this town. It's time for him to think of himself and come live with his family."

Glancing down at his feet, Finnie dragged a boot toe across the boardwalk. He looked up, smiling warmly at Kate. "We want different things for Doc, but that doesn't make us enemies. That old cuss will do as he pleases no matter what any of us wants or thinks anyways."

"I expect you are right," John said before the stage driver began passing down the baggage.

With their belongings gathered, Finnie helped the family carry the load to the hotel and into their rooms. He started to excuse himself, but before he could finish, John invited him to walk with them to the doctor's office. As they proceeded down the street, Kate was forced to hold the hand of her youngest child, Tad, to keep him from bolting ahead of the rest of them. Rose, the feistiest of the children, had to be reminded to slow her pace as she skipped down the walk. She could barely contain her excitement in anticipation of seeing her grandfather. The oldest child, Henry, walked quietly behind the rest of his family in his normally reserved manner.

"Finnie, go inside and lure Father out here," John said.

"What should I say?" Finnie asked.

"I've never known you to be at a loss for words on any subject, and some of it, I'm pretty sure comes purely from your imagination. Think of something."

Walking into the doctor's office, Finnie found Doc taking inventory of his supplies.

As Doc looked over at the deputy, he picked up a scalpel and pointed it at Finnie. "Don't you start in on me over thinking about moving to Boston or I'll castrate you on the spot," he said as he shook the instrument.

"See, there you go being mean when that's not what I wanted at all. There's a family of Indians outside that wants to see you," Finnie lied.

"Really? Well, tell them to come in here. I'll treat them the same as any other patient."

"They refuse to come into the office. They want you to see them outside."

"Why in the world is that?"

Growing exasperated, Finnie said, "How would I know? They're Indians. You know how they love the outdoors."

"For goodness sake, I hope they don't want me to deliver a baby. That would be quite a sight on the street," Doc said as he walked towards the door with Finnie.

As the doctor stepped outside, the family yelled in unison, "Surprise."

Startled, Doc jumped back and looked dumbfounded at the realization that his family stood before him. "For the love of money, I can't believe it," he said as his eyes began to tear up.

John embraced his father and patted him on the back. "The family couldn't go any longer without seeing you. You made quite the impression on their first visit."

The doctor used his hands to wipe his eyes. "I guess I'm getting all misty in my old age."

"This has to be a shock," Kate said.

Doc made sure to hug each of his family members. "This is the nicest surprise in my life. My, you kids have grown. Rose you've become a young lady."

As the family followed Doc into his office, Finnie walked across the street to the jail. An hour passed while John and his family told Doc of their travels to Last Stand and other events in their lives. Rose, with her vivacious personality, talked the most. She charmed her grandfather on subjects as varied as the latest styles in dresses to her favorite subjects in school.

Finally, Kate stood and said, "I want to go see Mary and Sam. I love holding a baby."

"Let's head to the jail. I don't know if Mary is at the saloon or home. Finnie can tell us," Doc said.

Gideon and Finnie were sitting in the jail when the procession entered. The sheriff stood and warmly greeted the family. Kate insisted that Gideon catch her up on the news of his own family.

Growing impatient waiting for Gideon to finish talking, Doc said, "Kate wants to see Mary and Sam. Is Mary at the saloon?"

Glancing at the clock, Finnie replied, "She should still be at home. I'll walk everybody down there."

John stood and put on his hat. "I was hoping that the men could then walk to the Last Chance and have a beer. Henry is eighteen now. I can't think of a better place than the saloon where I got shot to have his first beer," he said as he retrieved the bullet from his pocket and held it up for all to see.

Kate rolled her eyes. "We all know the story. Please don't tell us again. You two can only go there on the condition that the sheriff and deputy are sitting at the table with you," she said with a laugh.

On John's first visit to Last Stand, a stray bullet from a fight over a card game had hit his chest and nearly killed him. Doc had learned that John was his son as he was about to perform surgery to save the man's life.

Gideon accompanied the others to Finnie's house where everyone crowded into the living room. Kate picked up Sam and began entertaining him as she and Mary reunited as if they had known each other all their lives.

"Let's let the ladies have some time together," Finnie said in hopes of leaving the confines of the overcrowded room.

After the men had left, Kate said, "I riled Finnie up when he found us getting off the stage. I told him we were here to take Doc home and you could see that it really upset him."

"You have to understand that we all think of Doc as family, too, especially Finnie. He's never said so, but I think he thinks of Doc as a father figure," Mary said as she began heating water for tea.

Kate took a seat at the table and began bouncing Sam on her knee. "Was he not close to his father?"

"No, they were very close. His father taught Finnie how to box. I think he misses those times and Doc helps fill that void. I know they make an unlikely pair, but it works somehow nonetheless."

Smiling at the thought of the two men sitting together arguing over just about any subject they could find to talk about, Kate said, "They do make for an odd pair. I don't imagine any of us will get Doc to do what he doesn't want to do. I guess we'll just see how it plays out, but I sure would love to have him with my children all the time."

∞

Finnie grandly led the way through the door of his wife's saloon. As the men took seats at Gideon's usual table, Doc motioned for Delta to bring five beers. Henry looked awestruck as he gazed around the room, enthralled with the sights, sounds, and smells of a real western saloon. While they waited for the beers, John pointed out the spot that he had been sitting the night that he got shot and recalled how he had to tell Doc just before surgery that he was the doctor's son.

After the beers were delivered, John said, "I'd like to make a toast to Henry. Son, you're now a man and a fine one at that. Remember with adulthood comes the responsibility to always do the right thing and to treat all things in life with the same respect that you would like to receive in return."

The men clinked their glasses and took a sip. Henry's face puckered up and he squinted his eyes shut as he shuttered. "This is what I've been waiting to try? Do you really like the taste of beer?" he asked to no one in particular.

"We Irish take to beer as soon as we are weaned off the tit, but I dare say for most others that it is an acquired taste," Finnie said before taking a big gulp to make his point.

"It'll grow on you. Just nurse it down," Gideon said.

Henry took a second drink and managed not to make a face this time. "That tasted a little better."

Looking at his son, John said, "Henry, are you ready to tell your granddad the big news?"

The young man grinned impishly and looked toward Doc. "I've decided to go to college to become a doctor. I've been thinking of nothing else ever since I helped you treat the gunshot wound on the blacksmith."

Doc slapped the table. "This day couldn't get any better. It's so good that I'm even buying the beers today. You may have to move out here and take my place. Nobody else seems to want the job. I certainly hope I live that long."

Finnie used his fist to pound his chest. "I don't know if my heart can take all this. I was surprised to see the family on the stagecoach, and to hear that Henry will be a doctor, but nothing is more surprising than Doc actually buying me a beer," he said and beat on his chest some more. "I may cry."

Chapter 6

As Finnie passed by the general store, he saw Rory Kasten loading his wagon with supplies. Finnie stepped up onto the boardwalk and began passing the bundles, wrapped in brown paper and tied shut with twine, to Rory to set in the buckboard. The deputy had met Rory only a few times, but the young man had made a good impression and Finnie liked him.

"Looks like you're planning to stock up for a good while," Finnie noted.

"Louise has a cold and didn't feel good so I came alone. I tend to buy more when left to my own judgement," Rory said and grinned.

"You better have something in those packages that she likes then to soften the surprise of all that you bought."

"I'm glad you said that. I meant to buy her some candy and forgot all about it."

"You take care, Rory. I'll see you around," Finnie said before walking away.

Louise had a sweet tooth and Rory liked to spoil her. He walked back into the store and bought a bag of chocolates before heading to the homestead that they could now proudly call their own.

The couple's property had been deeded to them the previous month when they completed all the requirements of the Homestead Act after five years of residence on their place. Rory had no designs on becoming a prominent landowner. He contented himself with owning enough cattle, hogs, and chickens to provide food and generate some cash.

During their time living near Last Stand, the couple had slowly gotten themselves acquainted with the community. They usually attended dances and socials, and over the last couple of years, had begun to attend the Methodist Church on most Sundays.

Rory surprised Louise with the chocolate as soon as he got home. His wife grinned at him like a child and gave him a hug before sitting down at the table to enjoy her treat. As far as she was concerned, bringing in the supplies could wait – chocolate should be savored.

While Rory walked to the door to go retrieve some of the goods he'd purchased, he saw three riders approaching. Though surprised to see company, the visitors didn't alarm him until they were close enough that he recognized their faces. Rory slammed the door shut and ran to his wife, yanking her out of her seat.

"The gang's found me," Rory said as he pulled a rug off the hidden door in the floor. "Get down in the hole and stay there no matter what happens."

Rory pried the hatch open and practically shoved Louise down the ladder into the pit he had dug before building the cabin over it. He hurriedly replaced the door and covered it back with the rug. Upon realizing he had failed to take the time to bolt the door, he ran for the entrance. The door burst open just as he reached it, catching him in the chin and chest. The force of the blow knocked him onto his back. Before he could recover, the three men surrounded Rory with revolvers pointed his direction.

"Long time – no see," Lester Cole said with a grin that flooded Rory with memories of the evilness of the man speaking.

Back when Rory had just turned twenty-one, he had crossed paths on the trail with the brothers, Lester and Greg Cole, and their cousin Howie Elkhart. They recruited him to help with a train robbery in Kansas. The gang had made off with twenty-five thousand dollars. Lester and Greg had each killed a passenger just for spite before exiting the train. With a posse on their tail, the gang had ridden to the Wyoming Territory before losing their pursuers. By that time, Rory had come to the conclusion that the others in the gang were idiots and meaner than a poked rattlesnake. He'd decided that he wasn't cut out for a life of crime and that the money would soon be pissed away, prompting the gang to commit more robberies. One night after the others had passed out from an evening of drinking whiskey, he had absconded with the money and all the horses. During the seven years since his escape, he had married and lived a quiet life in Colorado.

"How'd you find me?" Rory asked as he applied pressure to his split open chin.

Greg Cole reared his leg back, kicking Rory in the ribs. "I was sitting in the back of that saloon when you stopped in to have a beer today. My eyes about popped out of my head seeing you after all these years. Lester and Howie were getting barbered. We were just passing through town. I guess it was our lucky day."

Rory wrapped his arms around his sides and winced in pain as Lester stepped forward and towered over him.

"Rory, we can do this easy or we can do it hard. Where's the money?" Lester asked.

"That money was spent a long time ago," Rory said.

Using the side of his boot heel, Lester kicked Rory in the temple before looking around the cabin. "I'd think you'd have a lot more to show for twenty-five thousand dollars than this little shithouse. Now make it easy on yourself and tell me where you stashed the money."

"I tell you, I spent it," Rory said as he rubbed his temple.

Lester motioned for the other two outlaws to pull Rory to his feet. As they did, Lester pulled a cigar from his pocket and carefully lit it. He stood watching the others until he had the stogie drawing to his satisfaction. With surprising quickness, he smashed a right hook into Rory's jaw.

"Come on, kid. Don't make me do this," Lester said in tone that sounded like a father threatening his child.

Rory felt woozy. Only the two men's firm grasp of his arms kept him on his feet. "The money's in the bank in town," he lied.

Taking a puff on his cigar, Lester blew the smoke into Rory's face. "So let me get this straight. A hick from Missouri shows up in a town in Colorado and deposits all that money in the bank and nobody gets suspicious," he said before shoving the flame of the cigar against Rory's cheek.

Rory screamed in pain as the smell of his own burning skin filled his nostrils. "Go to hell. I'll never tell you."

"I hoped things wouldn't have to come to this, but you are going to force my hand. I happened to notice ladies garments hanging out on the clothesline. My guess is that there's a wife around here somewhere. I have no desire to hurt her, but if you don't answer me, I'm going to burn everything in sight. I'm betting I'll torch me a woman," Lester said as he watched with satisfaction as the fear spread to Rory's face.

"My wife is staying with a neighbor lady that just had a baby and is too weak to care for it."

Lester reached into his pocket and produced a match that he struck against his boot. He held it as it burned. "These cabins really go up in flames."

"Don't burn my home. This place is all that we got. The money's hid in the barn under a slab of rock. I can show you."

"Boys, drag his ass out there," Lester ordered as he dropped the match onto the floor and smothered the flame with his boot.

Greg and Howie walked Rory towards the barn as Lester followed with his pistol trained on his former partner in crime. Rory made no attempt to struggle, but walked as a man ready to face a firing squad with some of his dignity left intact. The slab sat near a corner of the barn hallway. Howie lifted the rock out of the way and reached into the hole, pulling out a metal box.

"How much is still left?" Lester asked Rory.

"A little over nineteen thousand dollars. We used it to get our homestead started."

"You didn't waste it. I'll give you that. You know, Rory, I liked you. For the last seven years, me and the boys have been living the high life with all the whores and whiskey we want, and we never worked a day for any of it. We've never been caught or even identified. The irony is that now you have to die and you only spent the share that you were entitled to get. If you'd only taken your share you wouldn't be in this fix," Lester said as he cocked the revolver, holding it mere inches from Rory's head.

Rory stared straight ahead into the barrel of the gun. He took a breath and released the tension in his body. Death would come on his terms. The roar of the revolver echoed against the barn walls as the shot slammed into Rory's forehead, sending blood and tissue flying through the air like a rain mist.

Chapter 7

Joann gave Zack a kissing before climbing up on the buckboard that he had just hitched up for her. She was off to watch Winnie and Chance so that Abby could go to town to visit with Sarah and Mary. The three women had resumed their Wednesday get-togethers now that the winter had passed. The day was warm with a nice breeze, and the sun shining on Joann's face felt good. She was excited to spend some time with her siblings. While following the road that led to her parent's house, she sang songs as she traveled and spotted some elk off to the north grazing on the side of a foothill.

Abby sat swinging on the front porch watching Chance chase the dog around the yard as Joann pulled up into the yard.

"You're looking pretty today," Abby said as she walked down the steps into the yard.

Joann scooped up her little brother as he ran to greet her. "It's too beautiful of a day for sulking."

"I suppose so. Winnie should be back from school by the time I return."

"I sure hope so. I want to spend some time with her, too. I feel like I've neglected both of them."

"They've missed you, but nothing that a little spoiling won't make up for."

"Abs, will you walk with me to Tess's grave?"

Tess lay buried beside Gideon's mother in the family plot. Since the burial, Joann had avoided even looking towards the grave site anytime she visited her parents, but today she needed to see Tess's grave. She felt as if her dark days were fading away much like the winter they had just experienced.

"Sure. Come on and let's walk out there," Abby said as she placed her arm around her daughter's shoulders.

Abby opened the wrought iron gate and followed Joann inside the family plot. Seeing the lime headstone for the first time, Joann passed Chance to Abby before lightly touching the marker as if it might be hot. Joann's eyes welled up with tears as she looked over at her mother and smiled through her pain.

"It's a nice little headstone and it's so peaceful here. I'm glad Ethan convinced us to bury Tess with my grandmother," Joann said.

"Thank goodness somebody was thinking straight during that time. The rest of us sure weren't," Abby reminisced.

"Do you really think there's a Heaven where we'll all reunite someday?"

Studying her daughter for a moment before answering, Abby said, "I do. I'm not so sure about all the details, but I do know that people have souls and that must mean there's a higher power than us. I don't know why God lets little babies like Tess die, but I think we have to trust in the Lord."

"I think you're right. There were days when I didn't believe in anything, but after Zack showed up and nearly got himself killed, I realized that God had given me a second chance. If he hadn't gotten shot, I doubt I'd be standing here today. I sure tried to run him off."

Zack had arrived unannounced up in the Wyoming Territory and surprised Joann. She had run him off and highwaymen had shot him as he rode towards town. He had nearly bled to death and had convalesced at her adoptive parent's ranch. During his recovery, Joann had decided to return to Colorado with her husband.

"We both know that life is unpredictable, but you're a survivor just like your daddy. You and Gideon might take a while to figure out things, but you both eventually get there," Abby said.

Joann chuckled. "I got there a whole lot quicker than he did."

"I have to get to town or Sarah and Mary will have all the cookies eaten," Abby said with a laugh.

After Abby left, Joann sat down beside the grave with Chance in her lap and talked to the grave. She gave Tess the whole history of what had gone on in her and Zack's life since the child's death. When she finished, she kissed her fingers and touched the gravestone.

"Let's go play," she said to Chance before walking back to the yard.

The two siblings played until Chance collapsed in exhaustion and fell to sleep in Joann's arms. She tucked him into bed and walked out onto the porch to relax. The time had gotten away from her and she looked up in surprise as Winnie walked up the driveway. Winnie saw Joann and ran to the porch, plopping down beside her sister on the swing.

"How was your day?" Joann asked.

"Good. I didn't get into trouble for talking or anything," Winnie answered.

Winnie had just celebrated her twelfth birthday. Joann looked at her and realized that her sister wasn't a little girl any longer. She enjoyed that she could now have more adult conversations with Winnie, but a part of her missed the little girl that had idolized her and followed her everywhere.

"That's good. Have you kissed Benjamin lately?" Joann teased.

"No, but I plan to one of these days. I'm going to marry him," Winnie announced.

"What does Benjamin think about that?"

"We haven't talked about that, but we're always together. I can't imagine that he won't want the same," Winnie said matter-of-factly.

Joann let out a chuckle. "I admire your confidence, Winnie."

Winnie grew quiet and introspective, and Joann could tell that something momentous was on her mind.

"I really miss Tess. It was fun being an aunt, and I loved holding her. Will you ever have another baby?"

The question caught Joann completely off guard and her eyes teared up again. She smiled at Winnie. After Tess's death, she had sworn that she would never go to bed with Zack again just to make sure that a child would never be conceived, but that had fallen by the wayside when they reunited. Another baby certainly was no longer out of the question, and for the first time since Tess died, the idea of another child no longer seemed frightening.

"I might someday. I don't know for sure," Joann replied. "You can help me take care of it if I do."

Chapter 8

Mounting his old horse, Monty Franklin had to coax it to move. The animal walked stiffly and occasionally stumbled from dragging its hoofs. Rory Kasten had promised to bring him a gelding that he was willing to sell, but he had never showed up, and Monty planned to get to the bottom of things. Monty liked Rory, even if he did so begrudgingly. The two men had nearly identical homesteads with approximately the same number of cattle, pigs, and chickens, but somehow Rory seemed to be more prosperous. Rory's wife always wore nice dresses and bonnets. Monty's wife made sure to bring the clothes to his attention anytime she saw Louise. Rory had nice guns too – a Colt Peacemaker, a Winchester 73, and a Colt 1878 double barrel twelve-gauge shotgun. Monty still carried an old Colt 1851 Navy with too much play in the cylinder, a well-used Winchester 1866, and a shotgun with no markings whatsoever.

When Monty rode up to Rory's place, he found it peculiar that the door to the cabin stood wide open. He poked his head into the home, but didn't see a soul. As he walked out into the yard, he called out Rory's name to no avail. He also thought it odd that the buckboard was loaded with supplies. Based on all the horse manure on the ground, he knew the animal had been standing there a good while. Growing uneasy, Monty walked to the barn. He smelled death before his eyes adjusted to the dim light in the barn and he spotted Rory sprawled on the ground at the end of the hallway.

When Monty neared the body, his stomach got queasy as the smell grew stronger. The sight of the flies covering the blood soaked face proved to be the last straw and he began retching until his belly emptied of lunch.

Monty ran out of the barn as fast as his legs would carry him, knowing he had to go get the sheriff. The gelding he had planned to buy stood in the corral. The horse could get to town twice as fast as his old nag so he saddled him and put the animal into a lope all the way to town. Gideon and Finnie were sitting in front of jail smoking cigars when Monty pulled the horse up hard in front of them, sending dust drifting their way.

"Monty, we're trying to enjoy our smokes. We don't need dirt in our nostrils to accomplish that," Finnie said as he swatted at the dust.

"I just came from Rory Kasten's place and I found him dead in the barn. He has a bullet hole in his forehead. From the smell of things, he's been dead awhile. Louise is nowhere to be found," Monty rambled.

The news brought Gideon and Finnie to their feet.

"I just helped Rory load his buckboard with supplies two days ago," Finnie remarked.

"The wagon's in front of their cabin with the supplies still in it."

"I would say that gives us a pretty good idea of when he died. Did Rory and Louise feud much?" Gideon asked.

"Not that I know of. I've been around them a fair amount and they've always seemed happy to me," Monty answered.

"Finnie, go get your horse out of the stable. We need a second murder on our hands about as much as Rory needed another hole in his head," Gideon remarked.

Monty rode with the sheriff and deputy towards the Kasten homestead. He seemed traumatized from the ordeal and talked of the condition of Rory's body in great detail as they traveled. Once they arrived, Monty said, "I borrowed this horse to get to you quickly. I was supposed to buy him from Rory. Do you think I could give you the money and just keep him?"

"I don't think that would be a good idea until we get things figured out here. You better take your horse and go on home," Gideon said. "Thanks for coming to get us."

The lawmen waited until Monty returned the horse to the corral and rode away before they walked into the barn. The buzzing of the flies in the otherwise still barn sounded like a beehive. Opening the rear door to shed more light, Gideon looked down at the body for the first time.

"Well, I think we can rule out Louise killing him. Somebody worked him over," Gideon said as he used his hat to fan away the flies.

Squatting down, Finnie studied Rory's face. "It looks like they burned him with a cigar to me"

"And they probably have a two day head start on us if they're running. Let's see if we can figure anything out in the cabin."

"I didn't know Rory well, but he seemed like a nice enough chap," Finnie said as he stood.

Gideon began to take a step away from the body when he noticed the hole in the dirt and the slab rock. "Rory had something hid out here and somebody knew about it. It looks like they were willing to murder to get it."

"I never would have figured Rory for one with secrets."

"Sometimes you just never know," Gideon said before walking out of the barn.

As they walked towards the cabin, Finnie looked up at the sky. "I wonder if Louise is still alive. I don't see any buzzards flying around. That's a good sign."

"Yeah, it is, but I fear that whomever did this took her," Gideon said as he stepped up on the porch.

As they walked into the cabin, Finnie spotted a few drops of blood on the floor and pointed at them. "Looks like it all started in here."

"So it would seem," Gideon said as he walked past the blood and looked into the other rooms of the house.

"See anything?" Finnie asked upon Gideon's return.

"Not a thing," Gideon replied as he walked past the kitchen table.

The light shining across the floor from the still open door gave Gideon pause. He noticed a strip of wood a couple of inches from the rug that wasn't as dusty as the rest of the floor as if the rug had been replaced in a different spot. Gideon yanked the mat away and found the door. With his knife, he quickly pried it up. When he lifted the hatch away, he could just make out the form of Louise in the dim light.

"Louise, this is Sheriff Johann. Are you hurt?"

"No."

"Can you climb out of there?" Gideon questioned.

Louise climbed the ladder and Gideon helped pull her out of the hole.

"I need some water," Louise said as she squinted and held her hands up to shade her eyes from the light.

Finnie walked to a bucket sitting by the stove and used a tin can to dip her out some water. Louise noisily drained the can in one long drink.

"How long have you been down there?" Gideon asked.

"I don't know. Ever since Rory saw the gang riding up. I was afraid to come out of the hole. Where is Rory? Did they take him?"

Gideon and Finnie exchanged glances.

Fearing that Louise would become inconsolable after learning of Rory's death, Gideon decided to try to get some information from her first. "Have a seat, Louise. I'm sure you don't feel well, but I need you to explain to me what happened. Time is of the essence."

Sitting down, Louise eyed Gideon for a moment as she contemplated what to say. Living a lie didn't seem to be an option any longer. "Before I met Rory, he joined a gang that robbed a train. He decided once was enough for him, but before he ran off, he stole all the money from the gang. That's why we always had money for a few nice things. We had over nineteen thousand dollars still hid in the barn. Rory saw them riding up whatever day that was and had me hide in our pit under the floor."

"Louise, do you know the names of the men in the gang?" Gideon asked.

"Rory wrote out a confession with all the details in case this ever happened. He always said the gang would kill him if they found him. He's been looking over his shoulder for a long time. It's tucked in the family Bible. Did they take Rory?" Louise demanded.

"Where is the Bible?" Gideon asked.

Pointing to a table, the Bible sat beside an oil lamp. Gideon walked over and flipped through the pages until he found a sheet of paper neatly folded and tucked between the pages. He retrieved the note and shoved it into a pocket without bothering to look at it. Turning to Louise, Gideon said, "I'm truly sorry for your loss, but Rory is dead."

Louise let out a scream that hurt both men's ears. She buried her face in her arms on the table, crying uncontrollably and mumbling indecipherably, for what seemed like forever. Gideon and Finnie stood useless, exchanging helpless glances, and waited until the woman had cried herself out.

When Louise raised up her head, she said, "I knew tainted money would be our ruin. No good can come from such." She stood up before collapsing back into her chair. "I'm feeling faint."

"You have to be dehydrated and hungry," Finnie said as picked up the can and refilled it with water.

Louise gulped the water down again. "Thank you."

"I'm fixing you something to eat," Finnie said.

While he waited for the stove to heat, Finnie found the supply of eggs and bacon. He began frying the food and humming an Irish lullaby as he worked. When he had finished, he brought the plate of food with another can of water to the table and sat down with Louise as she ate.

Gideon had never been good with dealing with idle time. He had unloaded the wagon of the supplies and brought the things into the cabin to keep himself occupied. After he finished, he walked back out onto the porch and pulled Rory's confession from his pocket.

Unfolding the paper, the note was written out in extremely neat block letters that made for easy reading. Gideon remembered hearing of the train robbery that had long been attributed to the James' gang. The confession detailed each man's name and their role in the robbery as well as their hometowns. All of the men except for Rory were from farmland outside of Fayetteville, Arkansas. Seeing the name of the town gave Gideon a jolt. He and Finnie had fought in the war with the Second Colorado Cavalry near there. Carefully refolding the paper, Gideon put the note back into his pocket and went inside the home.

A few minutes later, Monty Franklin and his wife walked into the cabin. Louise ran to Mrs. Franklin and the two women embraced. Mrs. Franklin patted the young woman's back and attempted to comfort her as Louise began wailing again.

"I thought I better come back to take care of the livestock. I didn't know if you'd still be here or not. The misses insisted on coming with me in case a woman might be needed. I'm sure glad you found Louise," Monty said.

"I'm relieved you returned," Gideon remarked.

"Sheriff, I'm sure you have things you need to do if you're finished here. I will go get a couple of other neighbors to help out Louise and take care of the body," Monty said.

"I appreciate it. We certainly have our hands full. We best get to moving."

After the lawmen took their leave, Finnie said, "I never would have pegged Rory for a train robber. This is a sad affair. Where do we start?"

"I read the confession. We're looking for some men named Lester and Greg Cole, and Howie Elkhart. I've never heard of them. They're from Fayetteville, Arkansas. With their new wealth, I'm wondering if they'll head home to get far away from here," Gideon said.

Finnie gave Gideon an inquisitive look. "If they are headed that way, can you even make yourself go back there?"

During the war, Gideon, Finnie, and two other men were separated from the rest of their unit during a skirmish somewhere near Fayetteville. Gideon had heard rustling in the brush and fired his gun with the assumption that they were being attacked by Rebs. The shot killed a young boy. The tragedy had so racked Gideon with guilt that he had spent the next fourteen years running from his conscience until he had landed back in Last Stand by happenstance. Only then had he been able to put his life back together and move forward.

"I guess I won't have much of a choice if that's where they are headed," Gideon answered.

"That could bring back a lot of bad memories."

"I don't want to talk about it right now and I need some time to think. They may not be planning to go there anyway. Let's see if we can figure out which way they headed and then we'll go after them tomorrow. Another day won't make much difference and I need to see if Zack will fill in for us while we're gone. Cyrus Capello is liable to cause mayhem if I don't," Gideon said as he spotted three sets of horse tracks heading east.

Following the trail of the gang, Gideon and Finnie rode east for a couple of miles. The outlaws had avoided using the roads and had made a point to make a wide berth around any homes they encountered. Most of the land they traveled across was open range grasslands. The spring rains had greened the grass and made it tall enough that the trodden trail the men had made proved easy to track.

Gideon pulled Buck to a stop. "Let's get back to town. We know which way they are headed and I don't think we'll find them over the next hill," he said before turning the horse towards town.

By the time the men reached Last Stand, the sun sat well to the west and the streets were busy with afternoon shoppers and men ready to head to the saloons for their first drink of the day.

As Finnie climbed off his horse, he said, "I don't imagine that Mary and Abby are going to be any too happy with our departures."

"I expect you're right, but it comes with the job," Gideon said as he followed Finnie into the jail.

"I hate the thought of us hitting the trail."

"Me too. I bet I've spent half my life sleeping on the ground," Gideon said as he dropped into his chair.

"And that ground keeps getting harder every year."

"You won't get any argument from me."

The door to the jail opened and Antonio Cortez walked in with a bottle of tequila in each hand. "Good afternoon, my lawmen," he said with a grin.

"Welcome, Senor Cortez," Gideon said.

Cortez had moved his large sheep operation to the county the previous fall. His arrival, as well as that of the sheepherding Laxalt brothers, had nearly started a range war. Gideon had negotiated a delicate truce that had seemed on the verge of collapsing until the ringleader of the ranchers had ended up dead. The sheriff believed that other ranchers had decided to kill one of their own in order to preserve the peace though he could never prove it.

"I just received a new case of tequila and I wish to give you and Finnie each a bottle as a small token of my appreciation for bringing peace and prosperity into my life," Antonio said as he set the two bottles upon the desk.

"Thank you, Antonio," Gideon said.

Finnie grinned and picked up one of the bottles. "I've been hankering to try this stuff again."

"Well, your hankering is over," Antonio said with a chuckle.

"So is everybody still honoring our boundary lines and playing nice?" Gideon asked.

"They are as far as I know. I check on the Laxalt brothers from time to time and they seem to be doing well. Dominique is not much of a talker, but I gathered from my last conversation with him that they are doing well."

Smiling, Gideon said, "Dominique's English leaves a lot to be desired, but they are good men. I'm just glad we still have peace."

"I need to get back to the flock, but I just wanted to stop in to see you. Enjoy."

"Take care," Gideon said.

"Thank you and be careful," Finnie added.

Once Antonio had departed, Gideon picked up the bottle of the tequila and stuck it into his desk drawer. "I'm saving this until we get back. That sure was a nice gesture on Antonio's part."

Finnie handed Gideon his bottle. "I like that Mexican. Put mine with yours. I wouldn't want a headache when we head out in the morning."

Gideon arose from his chair. "I'm going to go have a talk with Cyrus and then track down Zack. Would you please go ahead and get the supplies we need so we can leave early in the morning? Let's take a packhorse this time. I have a feeling we have a lot of miles ahead of us."

"I'll do it. Give Cyrus my regards," Finnie said sarcastically.

Gideon walked his horse down to the Pearl West and tied him in front of the entrance. He walked inside to find a good-sized crowd of early drinkers. As Gideon walked past the bar, the bartender started to say something until Gideon gave him a look that caused Jimmy to avert his eyes. Gideon flung the door open to Cyrus's office, causing the saloonkeeper to jump in his chair.

"Damn, did you ever hear of knocking?" Cyrus yelled.

"This is just a friendly little visit. I thought you'd be glad to see me and we could dispense with the formalities," Gideon said wryly.

"What in the hell do you want?" Cyrus asked angrily.

"I have another murder on my hands. It looks as if Finnie and I will be gone for a while. My son-in-law with be in charge while we're gone. Zack is as big as Jimmy and knows how to fight. I suggest you be a good boy and mind your manners."

"Why would I do otherwise? Have you made any progress with the murder that apparently happened by my saloon?"

"No, I haven't. Seems no one saw a thing."

"That's too bad," Cyrus said with a touch of mockery.

"Just so I make myself clear. If something were to happen to Zack, I'd kill your sorry ass and suffer the consequences," Gideon warned.

"You know that intimidation doesn't really become you," Cyrus said as he pulled a cigar from his breast pocket and examined it.

"No, it doesn't, but it's the only thing that men like you understand. Consider yourself warned," Gideon said as he deftly swiped the stogie from Cyrus's hand. "Thanks for the smoke."

Biting the cap off the cigar, Gideon then spit it onto the floor of the office before walking out of the room. Once out on the street, he lit the smoke before mounting his horse and riding away. He put Buck into an easy lope and headed for Zack and Joann's homestead. The horse wasn't as fast as he once was, but he still had the endurance to go all day. By the time they reached the cabin, Buck had worked up a light lather.

Zack and Joann were sitting on the swing on the front porch. Gideon climbed off the horse and jogged up the steps.

"Looks like you two are hard at it," Gideon said.

"I've been helping Ethan all day and you know that he's not happy unless he's finding something to do. I deserve a rest," Zack said.

"What brings you out here?" Joann asked her father.

After explaining the current situation and the details of the murder at the Pearl West, Gideon said, "I need you to be in charge while we are gone."

"What if the judge shows up before you get back?" Zack asked.

"Just go talk to D.A. Kile and tell him we'll have to wait until the next time the judge comes to town. Neither Cyrus nor that whore that I need to testify is going anywhere and there's no need for you to have to get in the middle of that."

"Ethan isn't going to be happy," Zack said.

"You don't have to spend all your time in town. You can still help him some. I just need you to make your presence felt so Cyrus doesn't try to take over the town. Ethan doesn't have much choice in the matter. He'll get over it."

"Easy for you to say when you'll be hundreds of miles away."

Gideon grinned at his son-in-law, but said nothing.

Joann stood. "You should consider yourself honored that Daddy trusts you so much. I have to start supper," she said, giving her father a kiss on the cheek as she passed him.

"Just be careful with Cyrus and that bartender Jimmy. I don't think they'll give you any trouble but be aware of them."

Zack shook his head and sighed. "I'm going to have my hands full with this place, working for Ethan, and being a deputy."

"It's good for you – builds character," Gideon teased.

"You and your daughter have given me all the character I need."

"How's she doing?" Gideon asked.

"Good. She's getting better by the day. She even visited Tess's grave yesterday."

"So I heard. I couldn't be happier for the two of you. I'll see you when I get back. And be careful," Gideon said as he reached out and patted Zack on the shoulder before leaving.

Not wanting to wear Buck out with all the travel that they would be doing, Gideon rode home at a leisurely pace. By the time he finally arrived, Abby had gone ahead and fed the children. She looked none too pleased when he walked into the cabin. He quickly told her about the events of the day. Abby's mood softened until he mentioned that he would be leaving to track the killers.

Closing her eyes and folding her arms, Abby sat down in a chair. "Sometimes I hate that you're the sheriff. I knew it would be dangerous, but I never realized how often it would take you away from home. We spent so many years apart that I hate wasting our time now."

"I know. And believe me, I have no desire to be gone or to sleep on the ground. It just comes with the job."

"How long do you think that you'll be gone?"

"I really have no idea. They will have a three day lead on us if they kept riding, and I think they might be headed back to Fayetteville, Arkansas."

Abby shook her head and then glanced up at her husband as she remembered that Fayetteville was near where he had killed the young boy. "Are you all right with going there?"

Gideon pulled out a chair from the kitchen table and sat down across from his wife. "I want to talk to you about that."

"Winnie, take Chance to your room and play with him," Abby ordered.

After the children had left the room, Gideon said, "Even back before I came to Last Stand and forgave myself, I thought about going back and trying to find the family of the boy I killed. I guess I've always been too big of a coward to do it. That's why I've never mentioned finding them. Now it kind of seems like destiny."

"Nonsense. You are not a coward. I can't think of a worse thing in the world to have to do and I don't think you should do it. Too much time has passed and they might kill you or try to have you arrested. You'll just be opening up old wounds if you do find the family."

"They may have never even found the body and still wonder what happened to him. This way they would at least know the truth. And besides, I can finally put the last part of this ordeal behind me. It's the right thing to do and should have been done years ago."

"What about us? What if they kill you or you are convicted of killing the boy and hanged?"

"It would have to be a military trial, and with Finnie as a witness, I'd never be convicted. Nobody wants to relive that war anyway. I'll just have to take my chances with the family. Abby, it's something that needs to be done," Gideon said with conviction in his voice.

"I think you are making your family play second fiddle just so you can clear the last vestige of your conscience. I don't know what we'd do if something happened to you."

"Abby, I don't plan on letting anything happen to me. I'm certainly not going to stand there and let them shoot me. And you would be fine with String working for you. In another year, you'll be making more money with our cattle than I ever thought about making as sheriff. I'm telling you that trying to find the family is the right thing to do. You know it is."

Letting out a loud sigh, Abby said, "There's more to this than making a living. The children need a father and I need you, but I might as well shut up. I can see that you've made up your mind, and I do understand, but that doesn't mean I like or think it is the right thing to do."

"We're probably getting the cart before the horse. I don't know for sure that I'm headed to Arkansas or whether I'll even find the family if I do," Gideon said. "I do know that I'm about starved."

Smiling sadly with resignation, Abby said, "That's one thing that we can agree upon."

Chapter 9

The sky to the east barely showed the light of the coming morning by the time Gideon arrived at the jail. Finnie was nowhere to be found, but a stack of supplies sat on the floor ready to be loaded onto a horse. Gideon fired up the stove and made a pot of coffee while he waited. He had finished his first cup by the time the deputy appeared.

"I thought maybe you decided to retire and just stay in bed this morning," Gideon said.

Scowling, Finnie walked to the coffee pot and poured a cup. "You never said anything about starting out early. I'm normally always here before you are and I already got my horse and the packhorse tied outside. I didn't know we were owls that could see in the night."

"How'd Mary take the news of us leaving?"

"I can't say that she was happy, but being the optimist that I am, I find her behavior a whole lot more comforting than if she had done an Irish jig upon hearing the news," Finnie answered.

"I guess you've got a point there. I never looked at it that way. We'll head out when you finish your coffee."

"I went through our wanted posters and didn't find anybody by those names," Finnie noted.

"Their names sure didn't ring a bell with me."

"How do you think these outlaws have been robbing for at least seven years and nobody knows who they are?" Finnie asked before taking a loud sip of coffee.

"I don't know. They must be really good at planning and escaping. They also probably use aliases and nobody has learned their real names. We don't even know what they look like. Maybe we have posters for them under some other names for all we know."

"That's true," Finnie said before draining his coffee cup and then cursing for burning his mouth.

The two men loaded the packhorse, making sure to distribute the weight evenly on both sides of the animal before retrieving a generous supply of cartridges and shoving them into their saddlebags. The sun had climbed halfway above the horizon by the time they mounted their horses.

Gideon made a quick glance down the street. "I sure wish we were returning instead of leaving," he said as he nudged his horse into moving.

They rode back to where they had left the trail and resumed following the tracks. The grass had begun to recover from the trampling and required more concentration to spot the outlaw's path than the previous days. After riding for a couple of hours, they came to the road that led to Alamosa where the hoof prints disappeared in a barrage of other tracks on the well-traveled route.

"We might as well get on down to Alamosa and see if Sheriff White has come across our men," Gideon said as he nudged Buck into a lope.

Traveling to Alamosa took most of the day. Clouds rolled in as they rode and caused a drop in the temperature. The coolness made the horses frisky and willing to race. Gideon and Finnie would ride at a walk up the steeper rises and hold the horses to a lope when they encountered gentle downhill grades or flat stretches.

As they rode, Gideon told Finnie of his plan to find the family of the dead boy if they reached Arkansas.

"I figured as much," Finnie said.

Looking over in surprise, Gideon asked, "And how, pray tell, did you know that?"

Shaking his head, Finnie sighed. "Gideon, you are as predictable as a buck chasing a doe during mating season. I decided a long time ago that one of these days you would go back there to try to find the family. It was inevitable."

Pulling his head back, Gideon looked skeptically towards Finnie. "I didn't even know I would do this. So how could you have known? I wasn't aware that you could tell the future."

"Have you not thought about it for a long time?" Finnie asked.

Narrowing his eyes, Gideon said, "So you can't tell the future, you just read minds."

"Answer the question."

"Yes, I have," Gideon said with annoyance in his voice. "I know Mary thinks she can read my mind. I guess she told you."

"I don't mean to hurt your delicate little feelings, but Mary and I don't sit around talking about you all the time. Gideon, I've known you since both of us couldn't grow a good beard. You always eventually get around to doing what you think is right. The only thing surprising is that you didn't do it a long time ago."

Gideon sucked in a big breath and blew up his cheeks as he exhaled. As he rubbed his scar, he said, "I know. I guess I'm a coward at heart."

Finnie let out a snort. "That you are not, but you are mortal. Sometimes you forget that point. Nobody would cherish the job you have at hand."

The two men rode on in silence. They reached the town at suppertime and found a note on the sheriff's door stating that he was dining at the City Café.

"I guess we spared ourselves having a meal on the trail," Finnie said as they located the restaurant and began walking its direction.

"Eat up. I doubt we will be so lucky much of the time. We'd probably get fat if we didn't have to chase outlaws and nearly starve ourselves."

The two men entered the café. As eating establishments went, this one looked particularly well-lit and clean. The lighting and checkered tablecloths gave the place a homey feel that was rewarded by a near full capacity crowd carrying on animated conversations. Gideon scanned the room until he saw the sheriff sitting at a corner table dining with another man. Sheriff White spotted Gideon at nearly the same time and motioned for them to join him.

"Have a seat, gentlemen. How have you been?" Sheriff White asked as he motioned at the two empty seats at the table and proceeded to introduce his dining companion.

Sheriff White was a pudgy man with a soft appearance that didn't tend to strike fear into the hearts of men. His reputation as a lawman was middling, but he served his town well enough to hold onto his job. Gideon liked the sheriff and appreciated his past cooperation when breaking up a rustling ring that had used the rail yard in Alamosa to ship the stolen cattle.

"We've been living the good life," Finnie said before Gideon could answer.

The waitress descended upon the new customers and Gideon and Finnie hastily placed their orders.

"I don't suppose you rode all the way to Alamosa just to have a steak at the City Café," Sheriff White remarked.

"We're tracking three men that we think probably passed through your town. I was hoping that you might have caught wind of them. I don't even have a description of what they look like. They killed a man," Gideon said.

A curious look came over Sheriff White. "Well, I might have. Two nights ago, three men showed up late at night at the Alamosa Saloon. From what I'm told, they were spending money like it was water and buying the house drinks. They started to get rowdy and the bartender sent one of the girls to get me out of bed. I went in the saloon with a shotgun and ran them out of town. They didn't give me any trouble. In fact, they apologized and headed right out of town."

Gideon sat back in his chair and rubbed his scar. "I'd say that was our men. Can you at least give me a description of them?"

"Two of them must have been brothers. They looked a lot alike. Medium height and build, dark hair – really nothing distinguishing about them. The other one was shorter and stocky, light brown hair, and had a scar across his chin like maybe a horse had kicked him at some point. Oh, they all had southern accents too. I didn't see their mounts," Sheriff White replied.

"Well, that's more than we had. Maybe with a little luck we'll pick up their trail again."

"I wish I had known you were on the lookout for them."

"You had already run them out of Alamosa by the time that I found out about them. I appreciate the information."

The waitress brought the four men their meals. As they ate, Gideon and Sheriff White caught each other up on all the happenings in the area. Finnie did his best to add some humor to the monotonous conversation and kept receiving dirty looks from Gideon as if he were an ill-behaved child.

As the men paid for their meals, Gideon looked out the window. "We still have well over an hour of daylight. We best ride on and cover as much ground as we can."

Finnie had a look of disgust on his face. "You mean to tell me we're going to pass up a bed for the hard old ground when you know full well we'll be spending most of our nights in the outdoors?"

"The sooner we find them the sooner we get to go home."

"You remind me of the whore that insisted on taking one more trick before retiring for the evening and then woke up in the morning complaining how sore she was."

Rolling his eyes, Gideon said, "I'll use my time riding to try to decipher what that has to do with me."

Sheriff White shook the hand of each of the men outside the cafe. "Don't argue all the way there or those outlaws are liable to hear you coming from a county away."

"It's one of the perils of having an Irish deputy," Gideon said as he mounted Buck.

Chapter 10

After sitting in the jail for an hour going through the mail and sorting out a new batch of wanted posters, Zack decided he should make a walk of the town just so the townsfolk knew that he was the law if they needed him. He put his hat on and took a couple of steps when the door opened and Cyrus Capello entered.

Zack had never met the man and only recognized him from Gideon having pointed him out one time. The saloonkeeper looked even more greasy and sinister up close than he did from a distance. He gave Zack the creeps. Gideon had insisted that Zack be careful around Cyrus and try to avoid him if possible. Straightening his posture and pulling his shoulders back, Zack towered over the Italian even more than he normally would have.

"Can I help you?" Zack asked.

"I'd like a word with you. Can we sit down?" Cyrus asked.

"Sure," Zack said and returned to his seat.

After sitting down, Cyrus said, "I know the sheriff is out of town, but I wondered if there is any new news about the murder that apparently happened behind my saloon? Murders are bad for business and customers are asking me about it. I was hoping I could put their minds at ease."

Knowing that he was being played, Zack took his hat off and slowly sat it on the desk while he decided what to say. Gideon had made it clear that he gave Cyrus the impression that he had no leads on the murder. "From what I understand, the sheriff doesn't know the name of the victim or have any idea on the murderer."

"Your father-in-law doesn't seem to be as smart as he thinks he is on solving crimes," Cyrus said, looking Zack in the eyes to see if he could rattle him.

Zack smiled and met Cyrus's gaze head on. "I'm just glad that I'm on his side. I sure wouldn't want to bet against him."

"I've worked in towns before that had a sheriff like yours that thinks he owns the place and can do whatever he wants. Since the sheriff hasn't arrested me, I think it safe to assume I've committed no crimes because he makes his disdain for me quite clear. I've done nothing to warrant such treatment. People always get their comeuppance in the end. So will Sheriff Johann. " Cyrus said with a sneer on his face.

"Mr. Capello, I have no intention of sitting here and getting a lecture from you. If you have business with me, state it. Otherwise, get your greasy ass out of here before I throw you out in the street for all of Last Stand to see and talk about," Zack said and stood with his hands on his hips waiting.

Standing and brushing some dust off his black coat, Cyrus said, "I hoped that you would be of a more reasonable nature than the sheriff. I guess you have to kiss his ass to keep peace in the family."

Zack shoved his hands into his pockets to keep from going across the desk to pummel the saloon owner. He fought his inclination to show anger on his face and instead chose to stare Cyrus into leaving.

Cyrus sauntered across the room and departed without saying another word. As the sound of his steps faded away down the boardwalk, Zack sat back down and tossed his hat across the room in frustration. He had no idea if he had handled the situation well or made a mess of it. Confrontation was not something that he liked or felt the least bit comfortable in doing. Deciding that the walk of the town would be the best thing to calm himself, he walked over and picked up his hat. The door opened as Zack straightened up and he glanced over expecting to see the return of Cyrus, but instead saw Doc.

"I just saw Cyrus walking out of here and thought I should check on you," Doc said.

Smiling, Zack ran his fingers around the brim of his hat. "You might have to treat me for a stroke. Cyrus riled me up but good. I don't know if I handled it well, but I didn't let him push me around," he said.

"Then you handled it just fine."

"Gideon might not think so."

"To hell with what Gideon might think. You're the law until he gets back," Doc said with a grin. "He's been doing this kind of thing a lot longer than you have. And us that have known him forever know that he has some faults of his own. He can walk around all high and mighty, but we know that it's to cover his flaws. And besides, he wouldn't have put you in charge unless he trusts you."

Zack let out a laugh as he popped his hat onto his head. "Gideon would die if he knew you were talking about him like that."

"I love Gideon like a son, but just as Mary likes to tease him about being a legend, I like to take a pin and let some of that air out of him," Doc said.

Turning serious, Zack asked, "Do you think I'm going to have trouble with Cyrus?"

"I don't know, Zack, but I know that you are up to the challenge. Compared to losing Tess and dealing with Joann's grief, Cyrus is nothing more than a pimple on your ass. You tend to sell yourself short. Gideon sang your praises from the moment he brought you to Last Stand. I may give Gideon a hard time, but he knows men and he would have run you out of town before he let you marry his daughter if he didn't think you measured up."

"I planned to take a walk of the town, but you've made me feel so good that I think I'll buy you a beer down at the Last Chance."

"You know me – there are very few things I love in this world more than a free beer," Doc said and started heading towards the door.

Doc and Zack walked into the saloon and sat down at the table that Gideon always preferred for holding court. The Last Chance had a big afternoon crowd and the place was filled with noise and smoke. Mary and Delta were both working and taking turns tending the bar and delivering drinks to the tables. After filling two mugs, Mary brought over the beers and joined the men at the table.

"I can't sit long, but how could I resist the opportunity to spend a moment with two of my favorites," Mary said.

"Zack's buying me a beer. How about that?" Doc said and winked at the saloonkeeper.

"Well, I don't know of anybody that enjoys hoarding their money quite like you," Mary teased.

Knowing that Mary had her finger on the pulse of the town as much as anyone, Zack asked, "Do you know of anything around town that I need to concern myself with?"

"I do not. Everything seems to be pretty quiet right now. How's Joann?"

"She's doing good. Most days she's her old self now. There was a time there where I never thought I'd say that again."

"Joann is a strong woman. She just needed to figure that out for herself. Losing Tess was a lot for both of you to go through," Mary said.

Zack nodded his head and took a sip of beer. He appreciated the concern that others had for him and Joann, but there were days where he would have preferred not to talk about all that they had gone through. In his mind, the time had come to move on with their lives.

Mary sensed Zack's discomfort and decided to change the subject. "I wonder how Gideon and Finnie are making out. They're probably arguing every mile of the trip."

After taking a drink of beer, Doc returned his mug to the table with a thud. "If Finnie is part of a conversation you can pretty well bet that there will be arguing involved."

"You wouldn't have it any other way," Mary said.

"I suppose not, but don't tell Finnie," Doc said with a grin.

"I'm surprised that you are not out with your family."

"I need to leave here shortly. We're having dinner together tonight and then we are headed to my office for an evening of conversation. I've never told them much about my family. John and Henry are both curious to learn about some of their ancestors," Doc said.

Two men towards the back of the saloon began shouting at each other. As the yelling continued, it became apparent that one of the cowboys believed the other was messing around with his girlfriend. Neither man had risen from his seat or drawn a weapon, but a physical altercation seemed to be on the verge of taking place.

"I guess I better put an end to the argument," Zack said as he stood.

"Be careful," Mary warned.

For a big man, Zack moved stealthily between tables and chairs until he stood about ten feet from the still quarreling men. In a voice loud enough to drown out the others, Zack yelled, "You two men need to calm yourselves down or take it outside."

The man with his back to Zack spun around to see who had called them out. "Well, if it isn't the sheriff's little boy-in-law. I hear he has to ask permission from the sheriff to kiss his wife goodnight," the man said.

Not wanting to escalate things, Zack spoke in a calm voice, "Just settle things down."

"Just because the sheriff pinned a badge on you don't make you the law in my opinion, and I don't take orders from you," the man said and turned his head to grin at the others at the table.

"Do you really want to do this?" Zack asked.

With surprising deftness, the man drew his revolver and pointed it at Zack. "I also heard that you don't even know how to use a gun. Now if you want to live another day, you can slink back to your daddy-in-law and let him tuck you in bed," the man said and laughed at the deputy.

Zack looked around to size up the situation. All eyes were trained on him and waiting for his response. He had no desire to shoot the cowboy nor did he think he could draw his gun and fire before the man cocked and fired the gun already aimed his way. The only thing Zack knew for sure was that he wasn't running. As the man laughed again, Zack charged towards him like a bull on the rampage. The cowboy seemed too surprised to move or cock his gun. Zack delivered a downward right hook to the shorter man's temple that knocked him unconscious before he hit the ground.

As Zack drew his gun and cocked it, he pointed the weapon towards the men at the table. "I'm starting to get mad now and my knuckles hurt on top of that. I really don't appreciate how you all stood around to see what I was made of and let your friend make a fool of himself. You can all leave now or I just might shoot you so that I don't hurt my hand anymore."

The men jumped up from their chairs and headed for the door. Zack grabbed the prone man by the legs and began dragging him. As he neared the table where Doc and Mary sat, he stopped.

"That was either mighty brave or foolish," Doc said.

"It was brave, Doc," Mary said. "That's exactly what Gideon would have done."

Smiling, Zack said, "It seems that this is the day that everybody wants to test my mettle. I just might shoot the next one."

Chapter 11

Four days of riding had taken Gideon and Finnie well past land they had ever before laid eyes upon. Some of the travel had been slow going through rough terrain on trails that seemed to double back on themselves with mountain passes so steep that the horses labored to make the climb. Finally, they had reached Walsenburg, Colorado, staying the night in the town after having no success in tracking down anyone that had seen the outlaws. The next morning they had headed south, staying east of the mountains and making good time. After crossing one last mountain range, they arrived in the New Mexico Territory. They were traveling on blind faith and a lawman's intuition that they were on the trail of the men that had murdered Rory Kasten.

They came upon the town of Raton on their fifth day out and stopped for a few supplies. The clerk behind the counter gladly volunteered that he had sold goods to three men a couple of days ago that matched the vague descriptions that Sheriff White had given Gideon and Finnie.

"Sounds like we might have gained a day on them," Finnie said as they mounted up and headed east out of town.

"I hope so. They probably don't expect that we're coming after them and aren't pushing their horses," Gideon said.

"It sure would be nice if we surprised them before they get all the way across the Oklahoma Territory."

"Yes, it would, but I wouldn't count on it," Gideon said as he coaxed Buck into an easy lope.

The traveling became considerably easier the farther they got from Raton as the land changed to scrubby grasslands. They followed the trail for the rest of the afternoon, planning to stop early to give the horses a chance to graze on the grass.

As they came upon a large hill beside the trail, Gideon noticed wagon tracks going straight up the incline. "Look at that," he said as he pointed at the tracks. "I wonder why anybody would take a wagon straight up that hill."

Finnie turned his horse and followed the tracks a few feet. "There are horse tracks beside the wagon marks," he said as he sniffed the air. "I can smell something burned too. I don't think we're going to like what we find."

"We better go have a look," Gideon said as he turned Buck and began ascending the hill.

At the top of the rise, Gideon and Finnie pulled their horses to a stop. Down below was a dry ravine with the remains of a burned out wagon. Little curls of smoke still floated up from the wood. Pots and pans were strewn about and the legs of a man protruded from under a bush.

Neither man spoke, but simultaneously nudged their horses down the grade. As they neared the bottom, the sight before them made it obvious that the wagon belonged to a peddler. The amount of burned and charred goods looked to be adequate to fill a store. While climbing down from their horses, Gideon and Finnie heard a moan coming from the man under the bush. Gideon grabbed his canteen as he and Finnie jogged over to the man.

"I'm Sheriff Gideon Johann. We're here to help you," Gideon said as he knelt beside the man.

"I'm Theodore Miller," the man whispered as he labored to breathe.

Theodore looked to be close to sixty years old. He was a plump little man with only wisps of gray hair remaining on the sides of his head. His shirt was drenched in blood from a gunshot wound to his chest. One leg of his pants had nearly burned away and his leg was severely scorched with skin hanging down that gave off a pungent smell.

"Here, take a drink of water," Gideon said as he held the canteen up to Theodore's mouth.

Taking a long drink, Theodore licked his lips when he finished. "Much obliged," he whispered.

"Can you tell me what happened?"

Moaning, Theodore said, "Oh, I hurt all over my body. I was traveling down the trail when I met three men. They pulled their guns on me and wanted my money. I gave them what I had – about twenty dollars. Then one of them shot me. He called one of the others by the name of Lester and asked what they should do. Lester climbed up on the wagon and shoved me into the back." Theodore paused for a moment from the exertion to catch his breath. "When we got to this spot, they turned my horses loose and set my wagon on fire with me still in it. They were laughing and making jokes about fried peddler as they rode away. I managed to get out of the wagon."

Gideon offered Theodore more water that he willingly drank. As the sheriff capped the canteen, he looked over at Finnie. The Irishman looked ashen, and as their eyes met, Finnie shook his head in disgust.

"Do you have family?" Gideon asked.

Theodore shook his head no.

"Finnie and I are going to take care of you. It's too late today to try to get help. In the morning, we will get you out of here. You certainly were out in the middle of nowhere."

Nodding his head, Theodore closed his eyes. "The railroads have about run me out of business. I thought I'd try somewhere new. I feared I had made a mistake the moment I got here. I've been robbed before, but nobody ever shot me," he said before drifting out of consciousness.

The two lawmen walked out of hearing range of Theodore.

"We can't move him. He'd be dead in an hour," Finnie said.

"I know, but I don't think he'll be alive come morning. I couldn't say that to him."

"I thought this bunch would be content to head home without causing trouble. I guess I figured that wrong. These are some ruthless men."

"We're going to get these sons of bitches. There was no call for this. Robbing is one thing, but trying to burn somebody alive is something entirely different."

"Sometimes it's hard to imagine the depth of depravity of some men," Finnie mused.

"Why don't you take the horses and stake them by that water we just passed. That spot had good grass. I'll get a fire going and fix some grub," Gideon said.

Finnie nodded his head and helped Gideon unload the supplies before leading the horses away. By the time he returned, Gideon had slabs of salt pork sizzling in the skillet over a fire of wagon wood. Gideon tried to get Theodore to eat, but the peddler refused food, asking only for more water.

As the sun set to the west, the temperature began to drop quickly. Gideon covered Theodore with a blanket, but the injured man didn't seem to notice and would only mumble nonsense when asked a question. Finnie busied himself with retrieving what wood he could find and throwing it into the fire before he and Gideon retired for the night.

They arose at the crack of dawn. Finnie went scouring about for enough wood to start a fire to make coffee, but found his searching futile. As he walked back to the camp, he saw Gideon digging a hole on the side of the hill with a shovel that had half the handle burned off it.

"I take it that he has passed," Finnie said.

"He has," Gideon said as he used his foot to drive the shovel into the ground.

The two men took turns digging until they had a suitable hole. They then carried Theodore over to the grave and lowered him in as gently as possible. Finnie made the sign of the cross and said a prayer before throwing a shovel full of dirt onto the body.

"Nobody but us will ever know where Theodore Miller is buried. I wonder if anybody will even wonder what happened to him or if he will be forgotten as if he never existed," Finnie said.

"I don't know. It makes you think though, doesn't it? I guess most all of us are forgotten in the end unless we left our mark on history. We can only hope that we left enough of an impression that a generation or two of our family and friends remembers us," Gideon mused.

"We're both going to be in a foul mood today."

"Not near as foul as we're going to be when we find those animals."

Chapter 12

Friday night found the Pearl West full of freshly paid cowboys with money just burning a hole in their pockets. They were loud and having a good time. Cyrus and Jimmy were both working the bar to keep up with the demand for drinks. The craps and faro tables were crowded with players, and men sat around two tables playing poker with the seriousness of an undertaker.

Fancy Broderick had just returned downstairs after turning her second trick of the night. She leaned her back against the bar and sipped a whiskey as she scoured the room for another potential customer.

Cyrus leaned close to Fancy's ear and said, "This is our kind of night. I bet the Last Chance is near empty. I'll put that damn saloon out of business yet."

Turning towards her boss, Fancy's face was inches from Cyrus's sinister grin.

"It's a good night," she agreed.

As she turned back towards the crowd, Fancy saw three ranch hands walk into the saloon that had been present the night that Andrew Moss had been murdered. They hadn't been back to the Pearl West since then and the sight of the men made her pulse quicken. She had tried her best to put that night behind her. Doc Abram had never mentioned her confession again and she knew the sheriff was off chasing some other murders. To her way of thinking, the whole thing was best forgotten.

One of the cowboys stopped near the door and grinned from across the room at the whore. "Fancy, we figured that you had either hightailed it out of here or was in jail by now. We all heard about a stranger getting his throat slit and you were sitting with the only stranger in here that night. Did he not pay for his romp? I'll pay for mine," the man hollered mischievously.

The man's voice had cut through all the racket in the saloon, causing the place to grow still with curiosity. All eyes turned towards Fancy.

"I don't know what you're talking about," Fancy said without conviction.

"Sure you do. You were sitting right over there with somebody none of us had ever seen before. You two looked like you were old friends," the cowboy said as he pointed at a table. "I was just kidding about you killing him, but I figured he's the one that got his throat slit. Weren't you at least able to give the sheriff his name?"

Fancy glanced over her shoulder at Cyrus. His eyes were narrowed to the point that they were mere serpent slits and his mouth was clenched so tightly that his lips looked misshapen. A chill ran down Fancy's spine as she realized that she was staring her own death right in the face. Cyrus would kill her as sure as the sun would come up tomorrow now that somebody had tied her to Andrew, and she knew he'd make sure nobody found the body this time. Her legs started running before her mind had even made the decision. She ran between the cowboy and his friend, shoving them as she bolted for the door. The jail looked dark and empty and so did the doctor's office. She began running for the Last Chance when she recognized Doc's slow shuffle coming towards his office. As she ran up on Doc, he nearly lost his balance from jumping in surprise.

"Doc, Cyrus is going to kill me. I'm not lying. You have to protect me," Fancy said with panick in her voice as she grabbed the doctor's arm.

Seeing the fear in her face, Doc didn't bother to ask questions but took her arm and headed for his office. He quickly unlocked the door and ushered her inside the building. Lighting a couple of oil lamps, he grabbed his Remington-Whitmore shotgun before sitting down at his desk. The excitement had his heart racing like a horse and he had to catch his breath before speaking. "Tell me what is going on?"

"A ranch hand came in that saw me sitting with Andrew that night and he bellowed it out for the whole saloon to hear. I took one look at Cyrus and knew he was going to make sure I never talked. I ran for the door," Fancy said as she paced the floor.

"You should be safe in here."

"You don't know Cyrus like I do. He'll be coming for me."

"I doubt that. If he came for you and you ended up dead, it would be kind of obvious that he killed you."

"I guarantee you that my body won't be found. They won't make that mistake again. He'll get all the other whores to say I ran away in the night. He's done that before. You can't convict him for murder if there's no proof I'm dead," Fancy said as she peeked out the window.

"Well, get away from the window then," Doc said gruffly.

"Doc, I'm scared," she said as she dropped into a chair and started crying.

"Go on and get in the back room. There's a bed in there. Don't come out unless I call you," he said as he reached into his drawer to retrieve a Derringer. "Do you know how to use one of these?"

"I do," Fancy said as she took the gun from the doctor. She scurried towards the back of the office.

The doctor laid his shotgun across his lap and scooted his chair up to the desk so that the gun was concealed. He lacked the patience to sit idly so he pulled out his ledger and began updating it to pass the time. The door to his office opened and Cyrus and Jimmy walked in before he had barely begun.

"Doc, I believe Fancy may have come here. She got upset and ran out of the saloon. I believe she thinks I'm mad at her, but I'm not. I'd just like her to come back to the saloon. It's a busy night and I need her," Cyrus said.

The doctor sat his pencil down and removed his spectacles. He wasn't in the mood to play games or to lie. "She's here all right and she is staying here tonight," he said matter-of-factly.

Cyrus seemed taken aback by the doctor's determination and hesitated before speaking. "I pay you good money to come check my girls every week. Do you really want to jeopardize that money?"

"First off, I don't need your damn money. I can live just fine without the income from you. Secondly, without me treating your girls, they'd be out of commission in no time flat and you would just be feeding them without making any money."

"She works for me and needs to get her ass back to the saloon. In fact, I more or less own her and I demand it," Cyrus said coldly.

"I believe we fought a war that ended ownership of people and I never knew it applied to white women in the first place. You best get back to your saloon."

"Jimmy, go back there and find her," Cyrus ordered.

The doctor, for his age, swiftly retrieved the Remington-Whitmore from his lap and leveled it at the two men as he cocked both barrels. "Not if you plan to live through the night."

Neither man moved so much as a finger. The silence made the tick-tock of the clock on the fireplace mantel seem loud and annoying as the time passed.

"You know, Doc, it's best not to point a gun at someone unless you aim to use it," Cyrus finally said.

"I've done it before. Back in the day, an outlaw that went by the name of Durango Dick showed up here wounded and brandishing his pistol in my face. After he repeatedly refused to put his gun away, I blew him clear out into the street. You can find him in the cemetery if you don't believe me. As hefty as you two are, I believe you'd only fly as far as the boardwalk, but you'd both be just as dead," Doc assured them.

Cyrus's face morphed into the look of a rattlesnake ready to strike, but he still didn't make a move. "Come on, Jimmy, let's go. This isn't over with yet," he said as he backed out the door with Jimmy following him.

When the sound of their boots clonking on the boardwalk faded away, Doc uncocked the shotgun and got up to lock the door and pull the curtains shut. "They're gone. You'll be safe tonight. Now try to get yourself some sleep," he hollered.

"Thank you, Doc."

The doctor sat back down at his desk. Smiling at the thought of his performance, he felt amazingly calm considering what had just transpired. He guessed he had reached the age where he didn't fear death or the likes of Cyrus Capello. After opening his bottom drawer, he pulled out a bottle of brandy and poured two fingers worth into his coffee cup. The liquor hit the spot and he nursed the drink for a good while. When he finished, he blew out the lamps and returned the Remington-Whitmore across his lap. A night of sleeping at his desk would be a small price to pay for feeling like a man still young enough to hold his own against an evil saloonkeeper. Leaning back into his chair, Doc closed his eyes and soon fell to sleep.

The next morning Doc woke up cold and stiff. He gingerly walked to the stove, throwing in kindling and getting a fire started. By the time the coffee began cooking, Fancy had emerged from the back room.

"Doc, I want to thank you again. I heard what you did last night and I'd be dead by now without you," Fancy said.

"You're welcome," Doc said, rubbing his chin and looking away in embarrassment.

"What happens now?"

"I'm hoping that Zack shows up at the jail this morning. I don't know if he will on a Saturday or not. If he doesn't, I'll send Blackie out to get him."

"What will Zack do?"

"I'm not sure except I know that he'll do right by you," Doc replied as he poured two cups of coffee.

The doctor pulled his chair over to the window and sat watching the street for Zack to arrive as he sipped his coffee.

"I've put you in a terrible situation. What if Cyrus tries to get even?"

"I'm not worried about him. If he does, he does. I've lived a good long life and I'd rather die for doing the right thing than die of old age just wasting away."

"I wish there was a way that I could fix you breakfast."

"If you're hungry, I have a few can goods. Not really breakfast, but better than nothing."

"I'm good," she replied.

Doc walked over to the door and unlocked it. He stuck his head out and yelled, "Zack, I need you over here right now."

The tall, big boned deputy walked across the street and entered the doctor's office. "What do you need, Doc?"

The doctor explained all that had gone on the previous night as Fancy added details. When Doc finished telling of the events, he added, "You're going to have to protect Fancy."

Zack dropped down on the bench across from the doctor. He used both hands to rub his face, tilting back his hat in the process. When he dropped his hands down into his lap, he looked as unsure of himself as Doc had seen him since his days of courting Joann.

"Doc, I have no idea what to do. It's not like I'm a real deputy. I'm just helping Gideon," Zack protested.

The doctor sat up straight in his chair and his face took on the appearance of a lecturing father. "Nonsense," he barked. "You most certainly are a real deputy. Gideon wouldn't have even considered leaving you in charge if you weren't. You might not have all the experience that Gideon and Finnie have, but you're certainly cut from the same cloth. Now quit feeling overwhelmed and think about what you need to do."

Zack looked up at the ceiling and let out a sigh before turning towards Fancy. "I guess I better get you down to the district attorney's office. You are going to testify against Cyrus and Jimmy, right?"

"I don't see where I have much choice in the matter. We'll all be lucky if we live through this," Fancy said.

Standing, Zack looked at Doc. "What am I going to do if D.A. Kile thinks I should go ahead and arrest Cyrus and Jimmy? I can't be here all the time."

"If I were you I'd deputize Blackie. He's trustworthy and dependable," Doc said.

"Can a deputy do that?"

"When you get right down to it, you are the acting sheriff. And it's a whole lot easier to seek forgiveness than it is to get permission. Just let me know if somebody gives you trouble and I'll take care of it."

Fancy set her cup down and stood. "I won't be safe even if those two are behind bars. Cyrus won't go down that easy."

"Let's go see the D.A. and then I'll worry about that," Zack said.

Drawing his revolver, Zack stepped outside. He looked down towards the Pearl West and didn't see a soul. Elsewhere, the walks were starting to fill with the usual Saturday morning crowd. Zack motioned for Fancy, and when she stepped out the door, he wrapped his left arm around her and shielded her as much as possible as they briskly walked down the street. The people on the sidewalks looked at him as if he'd lost his mind with his one arm around a whore and in his free hand he carried a gun. They made it to the D.A.'s office and Zack shoved Fancy through the door. The look on

D.A. Kile's face at seeing Fancy still in her saloon outfit almost made the danger worth the trip.

"Zack, what's going on?" Kile asked.

"I'll let Fancy tell you," Zack answered.

Fancy again told the events of the previous night.

When she finished, Kile asked, "So did you actually see Andrew Moss murdered?"

"I saw Andrew go into Cyrus's office with Cyrus and Jimmy and come out with his throat slit. I don't know which one did the killing," she replied.

"And you will testify to this?"

"I will now."

"I'll issue arrest warrants for both of them for murder. One's as guilty as the other."

"I guess I need to go ahead and arrest them then," Zack said.

"I think you would be better off. I would imagine that it will be safer to know where they are at all times and they can't run that way," Kile said.

"Sometimes I swear that Gideon is trying to get me killed," Zack mused.

"This is just unforeseen circumstances. We planned to wait until we knew the judge was on his way," Kile said.

"It might be my unforeseen demise. Can Fancy stay here until I'm done making the arrests?"

"Sure."

"If something happens to me make sure that Joann knows I had no choice and tell her that I love her."

"Just be careful so that I don't have to do that."

Zack walked out of the office and straight to the livery stable. Blackie was inside the barn going from stall to stall feeding the horses.

"Blackie, I need some help," Zack called out.

"What can I do for you?" Blackie asked.

"I need to make you a deputy to go arrest Cyrus and Jimmy. And then I'll need you to stay at the jail some when I can't be there."

"I got shot the last time I helped out Gideon," Blackie reminded Zack.

"I know you did, and I wouldn't ask you, but I'm in a fix. I don't know where else to turn."

"It's a good thing I like you and Gideon. This goes against my better judgement. I'm not much with anything but a shotgun."

"That's good enough. Let's get this over with," Zack said.

The two men walked quickly to the jail. Zack rummaged through Gideon's desk drawer until he found a badge that he tossed to Blackie. He then retrieved two matching double barrel Greener twelve-gauge shotguns and a couple of belts Gideon had recently purchased that held the shells. He handed Blackie one of each and then strapped on the belt.

"Do you want a revolver?" Zack asked.

"Nah, I'll stick with something that's hard to miss with," Blackie said as he checked the loads in the gun.

Zack and Blackie hustled down the street and crossed in front of the Pearl West. The blacksmith tried opening the door to the saloon and found it locked.

"Stand back," Zack said and crashed his foot into the door, splintering the doorjamb and swinging the door open violently.

Jimmy stood behind the bar drinking coffee in the shadowy room. He ducked behind it at the sight of the two men brandishing shotguns.

"Spread out," Zack yelled as he moved to the right and Blackie went left.

The bartender had his own shotgun. He hooked the gun around the side of the bar to take a blind shot. Blackie dove to the floor just as the shotgun roared. The shot went well above the blacksmith and blew out a window of the saloon. From the second story, the sound of the whores screaming carried down the stairs. Zack began maneuvering towards the opposite end of the bar while Blackie readied his gun from a squatting position.

"Jimmy, this is Deputy Zack Barlow. You need to surrender," Zack yelled.

Jimmy popped up over the top of the bar, swinging the shotgun towards where Zack's voice had sounded. Blackie stood and fired his Greener. The shot caught Jimmy in the face, driving him back into the liquor bottles behind the bar. As the clatter of Jimmy and the bottles crashing to floor faded away, the sound of scurrying out the back of the saloon caught Zack's attention.

"Cyrus is running," Zack yelled as he took off towards the rear of the building.

Zack made it out into the alley just as Cyrus reached the side street and turned towards the main thoroughfare. The deputy ran in pursuit of the saloonkeeper and reached the front street in time to see Cyrus riding away on a horse he'd pilfered. The deputy wasn't sure if the shotgun blast would even carry far enough to reach Cyrus, but he cocked both barrels and fired. Cyrus let out a yelp and the horse began bucking madly. The saloonkeeper sailed over the horse's head and landed on his stomach with a thump. He didn't move, but laid on the ground moaning as Zack jogged towards him. As Zack neared, Cyrus managed to get to his feet and produced a knife from under his coat. The saloonkeeper looked like a crazed wild man as he came charging towards the deputy. Zack grasped the Greener by the barrels and swung it for all he was worth as Cyrus plowed towards him. The butt of the gun caught the saloon owner across his left cheek and the side of the head with a sickening thud. Cyrus dropped to the ground in a heap.

Blackie jogged up to Zack. He bent over and braced his hands on his knees for support. "Sorry I couldn't get here quicker. I wasn't built for running," he said between gasps for breath.

"You did just fine in there," Zack said as he bent down to check Cyrus's pulse. "He's still alive. I thought I might have killed him."

A man ran over and retrieved the horse Cyrus had ridden. "You shot my horse," he yelled at Zack.

"I'm sorry. I didn't aim to hit it. Take the damages up with the county. I have work to do," Zack said in a tone to end further discussion.

"I guess we better carry him to Doc," Blackie said.

After recruiting a couple of men off the street, they carried Cyrus to the doctor's office.

"I see you handled things just fine," Doc mused as they placed Cyrus face down on the table.

Zack allowed himself to smile. "Cyrus might not think so and Jimmy definitely doesn't think so. Blackie had to kill him."

"All right, everybody out of here while I treat him. He's not going anywhere," Doc announced.

"Blackie, if you'll send the undertaker to get Jimmy, I'll take care of Fancy," Zack said as the two men walked out of the doctor's office.

Zack walked back to the district attorney's office. After telling the D.A. and Fancy what had just transpired, he and Fancy headed back to the Pearl West for her to retrieve her belongings. He noticed from Fancy's furrowed brow that the news didn't seem to bring her much relief.

"Unless Cyrus dies, this is not over with yet. I know him as well as anybody does and he won't go down without a fight," Fancy said.

"After I deal with Cyrus, I got an idea where to hide you. Can you ride a horse?" Zack asked.

Fancy smiled for the first time that day. "Riding a horse is nothing compared to some of the men I've ridden," she said and giggled.

Turning red with embarrassment, Zack left Fancy at the front of the Pearl West just as the undertaker and his men carried Jimmy out of the saloon on a stretcher. They had mercifully covered his body with a blanket.

Zack entered the doctor's office to find Doc standing at the washstand drying his hands.

"So how is he?" Zack asked.

"The buckshot barely broke the skin. You must have been a good distance from him. You fractured his cheekbone and he won't ever look quite the same. He has a concussion and is still unconscious. We'll just have to wait and see how he responds. He might be fine or he could die," Doc answered.

"Can I go ahead and lock him up?"

"Sure. I can check on him later over there."

Zack rounded up some men and they carried Cyrus to the jail. After locking the saloon owner in a cell, Zack walked to the livery stable.

"Blackie, I didn't take the time to thank you properly earlier. I am so obliged to you," Zack said.

"I'm just glad I could help."

Would you saddle me a gentle horse for Fancy to ride? I'm going to go hide her."

Blackie disappeared into the stable and soon returned with a saddled horse. Zack took the horse down to the jail to retrieve his own mount before heading to the Pearl West. Fancy stood waiting for him at the door.

"Let's get out of here. All the other whores are mad at me for all this. They fear the saloon will close down," Fancy said.

"We could only be so lucky," Zack said as he passed her the reins.

Riding west out of town, Zack and Fancy headed for Gideon's place. After finding only Winnie at the cabin, Zack headed toward where he thought the herd would be grazing. He spotted Abby with Chance on the saddle with her. She and String Callow were sitting on their horses on a ridge above the herd.

Abby had hired String Callow the previous fall to help her run the ranch. The tall skinny cowboy lived alone in a one-room outpost shack that Gideon and Abby had fixed up for him. String had proved to be an excellent hire and worked well with Abby. The solitary lifestyle seemed to suit him just fine.

As Zack and Fancy rode up, Abby did a double take at seeing the unfamiliar woman with her son-in-law.

"Abby, your husband has gotten me into a terrible fix. I had to go ahead and arrest Cyrus Capello and I need to hide Fancy. Oh, by the way, this is Fancy Broderick," Zack said before turning to Fancy. "And this is Abby Johann and String Callow."

"Oh, Zack, I'm sorry you have to deal with this. What do you need me to do?" Abby asked.

"I thought that we could hide her in String's cabin. Nobody would think to look for her there and there's barely a trail to that place. I doubt anybody could find it if they wanted to."

String stood up in the saddle, looking like a giant. "Now wait a minute. Nobody is asking me. I became a cowboy so I wouldn't have to deal with things like women," he protested.

Abby looked towards her ranch hand. "String, this woman needs our help and it would just be until after the trial. Gideon got Zack into this mess and I need to help him."

"But I only got one bed and I ain't sharing it with a woman," String complained.

Fancy turned her green eyes towards String and stared at him. "Don't flatter yourself. I wouldn't want to share a bed with your skinny butt anyways. I'd probably lose you in the sheets and smother you in my sleep. I'd rather sleep on a pallet on the floor."

The reticent cowboy was taken aback by the whore's words. He sat back down on his saddle and seemed to shrink in size. "Abby," he whined.

"String, we have to do this. I'll give you extra money for groceries. You'll just have to make the most of it," Abby said with authority.

"Come on. I'll take you there," String said in resignation.

"She'll have to ride with you. I have to return that horse to Blackie," Zack said.

String didn't say anything, but he looked at Zack as if he would like to kill him. He held out an arm and helped pull Fancy up onto the horse.

"Thank you for all you've done," Fancy said to Zack as she looked over her shoulder before they rode away

After String and Fancy disappeared from sight, Zack said, "Those two are liable to kill each other."

"She might be good for String. I bet she could teach him a thing or two that might change his mind about women," Abby said and started giggling.

Chapter 13

After days of riding, Gideon and Finnie were deep into the Oklahoma panhandle. Since burying the peddler, the travel had been uneventful and easy compared to crossing mountain ranges. The land had enough water and healthy grass to keep the horses in good condition and allowed the men to cover a lot of ground. They had crossed paths with a few people, but no one had seen the outlaws. One evening they had been lucky enough to meet a local rancher that had insisted they come to his place for dinner and to stay for the night.

Finnie had an extreme fear of Indians and constantly looked over his shoulder. He had once seen the bodies of a scalped family and the sight had left a lasting impression upon him. As they traveled, he would constantly talk about fears of being attacked by the savages until he had Gideon wishing that he rode alone.

"I don't know why you're so worried now. We haven't even reached the bad part of the Oklahoma Territory yet," Gideon said in an attempt to make Finnie feel as miserable as he was making him.

"That's just like you. You're just trying to rile me up more than I already am," Finnie said.

"Worrying won't change a darn thing. I don't know why you waste your time on it."

"Because I like my hair just where it sits now. A scalping would be a gruesome way to die," Finnie lamented.

"Those Indians would most likely kill you before they scalped you," Gideon said with a grin.

"Aye, that's reassuring. You have a mean streak in you that you fail to harness in your most vile moments."

"Riding with a blathering Irishman will do that to a man."

"You're like the whore that preached a sermon after she took your money and did the deed."

Gideon shook his head, but did not respond.

The two men rode for another half-hour without talking. Up ahead they spotted a rider coming their way. As he neared, they could see that he looked to be a young man barely out of his teens. He wore ill-fitting clothes with large patches on the knees of his pants and a hat that had long ago lost all semblance of shape.

"Howdy," the young man greeted them.

"Hello, I'm Sheriff Johann and this is Deputy Ford. We're on the trail of three outlaws. Two of them are brothers that look alike and the other is short and stocky with a scar on his chin. Any chance that you've come across them?" Gideon asked.

"I did yesterday morning. My name is Kenneth, by the way. They tried to rob me, but when I only had two bits on me, they laughed and said they weren't that desperate."

"You are lucky. The last man we know of that they robbed, they also killed," Finnie said.

"I think they thought about killing me. One of them cocked his gun. Then another one that looked just like him, but older, said that I was so poor that I couldn't afford to die. They all had a good laugh at that and then rode away," Kenneth said.

"Thanks for the information."

Kenneth grinned impishly. "I carry a five dollar gold piece in my boot. It's an old trick that my poppa taught me. Sounds like it might have saved my life."

"Take care," Gideon said as he nudged Buck into moving.

"Looks like we've narrowed the distance to a day and a half," Finnie said as they rode away.

"That's still a lot of ground to make up. We'll probably have to chase them all the way to Arkansas. It'll give you plenty of opportunities to spot an Indian or two."

"If I've said it once, I've said it a thousand times – Gideon Johann, you are a haughty man."

After riding another hour, Gideon said, "Let's make camp at the next water we find. We've covered enough ground for one day."

"Sounds good to me, but it looks like we may have company up ahead."

Three men had just topped a rise nearly a quarter of a mile away. Gideon's first inclination was to think that maybe the outlaws they were chasing had reversed course. He pulled his spyglass from his saddlebag and surveyed the men.

"Do you think it's our men?" Finnie asked.

"No, it's not them, but it's not a Sunday school class either. They look rough. Get your rifle out and have it cocked. Maybe there won't be trouble, but we'd better be prepared. Start shooting if I call you Finnegan. I'll be damn if I'll let them make the first move," Gideon said as he put his spyglass away and pulled his Winchester from his scabbard. He cocked the gun and rested it across his legs as they rode.

The riders continued on a straight course toward the lawmen. The three men were a ragtag looking outfit. Two of them were white men with scraggly beards and unkempt hair that stuck out from under their hats down to their shoulders. The third man looked to be a half-breed. He wore moccasins and a leather shirt with store bought pants. All of them were as dirty as if they had just emerged from a mine after a hard day's work. Each man had a rifle resting in his arms or across his lap. They rode to within thirty feet of Gideon and Finnie and stopped. The lawmen did likewise.

"This here is my road and you have to pay a toll to use it," the white man in the middle said. His two partners giggled and looked at each other with silly looking grins.

"I'd like to see the papers stating such," Gideon said.

"Out here we're not much for paperwork. A man's word is as good as the paper he's signed his name to."

Gideon looked the three men over trying to size up the situation before speaking. The two on the outsides were too amused with the proceedings to be paying attention. Only the one doing the talking seemed alert to the situation at hand. "We're a couple of lawmen from Colorado in the pursuit of some outlaws. We're not looking for trouble. Why don't you just let us pass?"

"I can see your badge and it don't mean nothing out here. Give us five dollars and you can be on your merry way. Otherwise, the boys are going to get ugly."

"So if you get your money you'll be happy to let us move on?" Gideon questioned.

"Now it's going to cost you ten dollars for wasting my time. I already answered you."

Rubbing his scar, Gideon sucked in a breath and blew it out loudly. He had no desire to get in a shootout with these men, but he also didn't think there was a snowball's chance in hell that they would let him and Finnie pass. This was all a game to these three men that they planned to play for their amusement and profit. Gideon reminded himself that when the time came, he needed to bring his rifle up level so as to not waste time lining up the bead on his target. He'd learned a long time ago that the little things could be the difference between life and death. "I think we better pay the man, Finnegan," Gideon said.

As soon as he called out the name Finnegan, Gideon brought his rifle up and fired on the man that had done all the talking. Finnie's Winchester roared a tick after his did. Without bothering to see if he hit the man in the middle, Gideon swung the rifle to the half-breed on his right. The man had jammed his gun in his haste to cock it. Gideon aimed dead center at his chest and fired. The half-breed flopped backwards in the saddle as his rifle flew through the air. Finnie fired a second round into the man on their far left while Gideon turned his attention back to the man in the middle. The first shot had hit the ringleader in the left forearm as he had raised his rifle up to fire. He now struggled to recover and aim his rifle with one arm. The two lawmen fired simultaneously, knocking the man clear out of the saddle. As the smoke cleared, Gideon and Finnie kept their Winchesters trained on the men. Only the half-breed showed any sign of life. He attempted to turn his horse, but slid to the ground as the animal moved and he lost his balance.

"You keep an eye on them while I'll check to see if they're alive," Gideon said as he climbed off his horse.

"Stay out of my line of sight," Finnie warned.

"Don't you worry about that."

Both of the white men were dead. The half-breed struggled to breathe. His chest heaved as he fought for air and his eyes stared with fear at the sky. He took a few breaths and joined his partners in death.

"Do you think I made the right call?" Gideon asked.

"I do. I was surprised you waited as long as you did. They were just toying with us until they got good and ready to kill us," Finnie replied.

"That's what I thought. Let's drag them off to the side and cover them with rocks. I don't know what else to do."

By the time they had covered the bodies with rocks, the sun was sinking low to the west. Finnie unsaddled the men's horses and turned them loose as Gideon piled the tack and guns beside the makeshift graves.

"Someone can come along and scavenge their belongings. These three won't be needing them anymore," Gideon said.

"Let's get to moving. You know how I feel about sleeping around dead people," Finnie said.

"I'm with you this time. If you are right about ghosts and such, I don't want to deal with those characters again tonight."

Chapter 14

Fancy Broderick had known a lot of men in her day – a lot of men. She figured she had bedded every kind of man that existed. From handsome to ugly, bold to shy, sweet to mean, and clean to disgusting, she had seen them all. There had been men that brazenly gazed at her naked body and others that were so timid as to avert their eyes. The one thing they all had in common was a need that only a woman could satisfy. String Callow was proving to be the one kind of man that Fancy had never before encountered – one so scared of women that he had apparently avoided them since becoming an adult. He acted so panicky in her presence inside the cramped cabin that she would go sit outside on the steps. The only time he acted comfortable is when he came home from work and she had supper ready. He would sit at the table with her and carry on like a normal human being. The moment the meal finished, he would avoid eye contact, become fidgety, and sweat would bead up on his forehead. Fancy would watch String and wonder if he feared she might strip bare-naked and have her way with him.

One night she couldn't tolerate the behavior a moment longer. "What is wrong with you? Every night you get all queer acting after supper. I haven't bitten you yet," she said.

"No, ma'am, you haven't," String answered as he stared into his lap.

"Well, then, what is it?"

"It's just – you know. You're used to having men all the time," String said quietly.

"What?" Fancy yelled. "Do you think that I need men like an addict needs laudanum? Don't flatter yourself. You may be tall, but that don't count for much in my experience. Bedding men is my job just like branding calves is yours. I don't get up each morning and start bedding men out of habit and I doubt you get up and go brand calves willy-nilly."

"No, ma'am."

"Quit calling me ma'am. My name is Fancy. Got it?" she shouted.

"Yes, Fancy," String said meekly.

Fancy looked over at String and knew she should take pity on him. He looked pathetic and miserable, but she hadn't said her piece yet and the pull proved too strong for her. A part of her was plain mad at his behavior and another part of her felt insulted that he had no desire for her. "You know, most cowboys would be tickled to death to be tucked away in the middle of nowhere with a whore, but not you. We could certainly pass the time doing something a whole lot more entertaining than having this conversation. Men do pay for me for a reason," she said before dashing for the door.

"Yes, Fancy," String said as she disappeared outside.

∞

After Zack woke up in the jail on the cot where his feet hung over the end, he slowly stood. He and Blackie were taking turns staying there. Zack frowned as he scratched his head. He hated being away from Joann and remained irritated at Gideon for putting him in such a predicament.

Shuffling his feet as he walked, Zack ambled to the cell room. Cyrus sat on his bunk holding his head. The saloon owner had been complaining of headaches ever since he regained consciousness. He looked like hell. His face was swollen, and black and blue to the point of making him unrecognizable. He looked up at the sound of the deputy entering the room.

"I'll go get you some breakfast," Zack said.

"Did they get my saloon back open last night?" Cyrus asked.

"They did."

"Thank God for that."

"I really doubt God cares about your saloon."

Ignoring the deputy, Cyrus asked, "Have I received a telegram from my lawyer yet?"

"Not yet. I doubt he wants to keep you from hanging any more than the rest of us do," Zack said. He had come to loath the saloonkeeper and liked to needle him every chance he got.

"This isn't over with by any means. You and that whore better watch your backs. I know lots of people," Cyrus threatened.

"I know of at least three people that would chase you into the bowels of hell if you ever try to harm me or anybody in our family."

"You think that sheriff walks on water. He'll get his comeuppance one of these days too."

"Big talk for a man sitting in a cell with his face rearranged."

From the front of the jail, Doc hollered, "Is anybody here?"

"I'm back here," Zack answered as he retrieved a pair of handcuffs from the wall.

Zack didn't trust Cyrus with Doc and insisted on handcuffing the saloon owner behind his back each time the doctor checked his patient. Cyrus stood and put his back to the bars. He had balked at being cuffed the first time, but after Doc threatened to withhold the laudanum for Cyrus's headache, he had acquiesced and never complained again.

Doc removed the bandages from Cyrus's face and applied iodine. The saloonkeeper winced and cursed under his breath as the doctor carefully reapplied the bandages.

"You're healing just fine. It's going to take some time for the swelling to go down. Have the headaches improved?" Doc asked.

"What do you think? You ever been laid upside the head with the butt of a shotgun?" Cyrus asked testily.

"I never tried to charge anybody with a knife," Doc answered as he handed Cyrus a small bottle of laudanum. "Make it last."

The doctor stepped out of the cell and Zack locked the door before removing the cuffs. He and Doc walked to the office and sat down at the desk.

"He threatened me and Fancy," Zack said.

"He's not to be trifled with. Watch yourself," Doc warned.

"I know. I'll be glad when this is over with. I sure wish that Gideon were here."

"Wishes are for blowing out candles. You're doing fine. Come on and I'll buy you breakfast."

Doc and Zack walked to Mary's Place. After enduring the usual onslaught of harassment from Charlotte, they ate at a leisurely pace as Doc talked about his grandkids and his plans to take them fishing along with the retired Sheriff Fuller that day. Zack, trying to put Cyrus out of his mind for a while, told the doctor about his plans for his and Joann's homestead. Once the two men had finished the meal, he carried a plate to Cyrus.

After delivering the food to the saloonkeeper, Zack grabbed the keys to the cells and locked the front door on the way out of the jail. He hung a sign on it before strolling down to the livery stable. Blackie stood hunched over with a horse's hoof between his legs as he nailed a shoe onto the animal.

"Blackie, I'm going home. I brought you the keys," Zack said.

The blacksmith finished hammering his last nail into the shoe before turning towards the deputy. "How are things down at the jail?" Blackie asked.

"Cyrus is as mean as ever. Be careful around him."

"Oh, I will. Don't worry about that. I'll be glad when I don't have to do this. I have my hands full running the livery and playing deputy."

"I know you do and I appreciate your help. I don't know what I'd do without you."

"Go ahead and get out of here. I'll keep things under control" Blackie assured him before going to retrieve Zack's horse from a stall.

On the ride home, Zack tried to put his worries out of his mind. He would succeed for a few minutes, but thoughts of Cyrus and the trial would start creeping back into his mind. The day was turning out to be the first really warm day of the year. He rolled up the sleeves of his shirt and tried to appreciate the weather and the view of the mountains for the rest of the trip.

Zack walked into the cabin to find Joann removing a pie from the oven. She quickly placed the dessert on the counter and gave her husband a hug and a kiss.

"I missed you and I made you a pie. It's kind of lonely out here all by myself," Joann said.

"I missed you too. We can thank your daddy for all this," Zack complained.

"Don't be mad at him. He didn't have much choice in the matter and you should feel honored that he trusts you enough to leave you in charge. You know full well that Daddy wouldn't do that if he didn't believe in you."

"I know, but it still makes for a worrisome situation," Zack said as he sat down at the table.

Joann sat down beside Zack. She noticed his furrowed brow and the tension in his jaw. Her husband looked as if he had the weight of the world on his shoulders. Guilt flooded over her. Zack's current worry might be over Cyrus Capello, but she knew that her handling of Tess's death had taken a toll on her husband. She felt sure that he would be handling the current situation a lot better if he had had more time to recover from all that she put him through or if she had never gotten so depressed in the first place. She wished that she could take his mind off his worries and make him feel special.

"I'll be right back," Joann said before she hastily retreated outdoors.

Zack sat at the table waiting for her for a few minutes. He assumed she had made a trip to the outhouse. After she didn't return, he decided he best go check on her.

"Joann," he called out from the porch.

"I'm down at the swimming hole. You won't believe what you'll find in the water," Joann yelled back.

Having no idea what Joann was talking about, Zack walked briskly towards the swim hole. As the hole came into view, he saw Joann standing naked in the water grinning at him like a Cheshire cat.

Back when she and Zack had been building the cabin, they had gotten into the habit of skinny-dipping and making love at the swimming hole to the point that it had proved a distraction to completing their home. All that had changed when Tess died. There had been a time when she could never imagine frolicking in the water again with her husband, but as she waited for Zack to join her, she realized that she wanted those times again not only to make Zack happy, but for herself, too. She had lived through the darkness and things looked pretty sunny now.

As Zack walked to the water's edge, Joann began provocatively gliding across the water away from him until she reached the other side.

"You should shed your clothes and jump in. They say swimming relieves tension," Joann teased before beginning her swim back to her husband.

"I thought I was going to get a piece of pie," Zack teased.

"Oh, I got a slice of pie for you all right."

As she made her way back, Joann giggled at the sight of Zack almost falling from shedding his pants in haste.

Chapter 15

The sun had just risen enough that Finnie could see well enough to find some wood. He got the fire blazing again and put coffee on while Gideon snored in his bedroll. They were well into the Indian Territory now and Finnie fell to sleep each night wondering if he would wake up scalped the next morning. He had insisted that they make camp the night before in the woods with the hope that their fire couldn't be spied from miles away. Just as the coffee finished cooking, Gideon arose and walked a few feet from the camp to take a leak.

"Dang, you'd make a good wife," Gideon said over his shoulder.

"You better get that thing back in your pants or I'm liable to make a wife out of you," Finnie threatened.

"Oh, Finnie, I wish we were home in our own beds," Gideon lamented.

"I know. I've been sitting here thinking about Mary and Sam. Maybe we should get out of this line of work and open us up a store together."

"And what kind of store would that be?"

"I haven't figured that part out yet," Finnie replied as he retrieved some hardtack and jerky from a pouch. The men had exhausted the rest of their supplies and were forced to subsist on the cold, dry food and the occasional cottontail or black-tailed jackrabbit.

"I'm not sure we're cut out for something that mundane," Gideon said.

"Mundane would feel a whole lot better than sleeping on the ground and eating this crap day and night."

"You do have a point there," Gideon said as he joined Finnie by the fire.

After washing the food down with coffee, the two men hit the trail just as the last of the morning shadows disappeared. They had ridden a couple of miles when Finnie started sniffing the air like a dog on a scent. "I smell bacon cooking."

Gideon inhaled deeply. "Damn, that smells good."

They came upon a little clearing where two men sat hovered over a campfire. One of the men worked at turning bacon over in the skillet while the other busied himself with retrieving the coffee pot from the flames. Both men looked up at the new arrivals, but didn't seem overly concerned. Rifles rested handily by the men's sides, but neither one of them made a move for their weapon.

"Howdy," one of them said.

"Good morning," Gideon replied.

"I see that you gentlemen are wearing badges so I assume that you have no inclination to do us harm."

"Can't say that we do."

"We have plenty of food. Would you have an inclination to harm some bacon instead? My name is Shad Nelson and this is Donnie Stahl," Shad said.

"We would," Finnie answered before Gideon could speak.

"I'm Gideon Johann and this is Finnie Ford," Gideon said as he climbed down from Buck.

"In case you're wondering, we're bounty hunters," Shad said. "We're up from Texas."

The two men stood and shook hands with the lawmen. Shad and Donnie looked surprisingly clean and kempt considering they had traveled from Texas. They had apparently stopped in a town along the way for a bath and barbering. Gideon guessed that both men were about his age and looked to have spent a lot of time in the Texas sun riding a horse.

"We're from Colorado and are pursuing three men headed for Arkansas," Gideon said.

Donnie began retrieving fried bacon from the skillet and placing it into a tin plate. He then forked more meat into the skillet, making the grease pop and crackle. Finnie watched the proceedings as if mesmerized as he loudly inhaled the aroma. By the time the second batch of bacon had fried, Finnie had retrieved their own plates and cups from the packhorse.

As Donnie distributed the food into each man's plate, he said, "It's nice to see a new face. We get so bored with each other that we ride for hours without talking."

"Aye, I know what you mean," Finnie said. "I can finish all of Gideon's stories for him."

Gideon let out a snort. "That's precious coming from you. You're the one that does all the talking, and I might add, repeating yourself."

"Sounds like you two have known each other a long time," Shad said before tugging off a bite of bacon.

"We met at the beginning of the war," Gideon said before taking a sip of coffee.

"We did too. I bet we fought on opposites sides though," Shad remarked.

"We fought for the Second Colorado Cavalry," Finnie said proudly.

"Yeah, we were Rebs. Those days were a long time ago and it doesn't much matter anymore on which side you were fighting," Donnie said.

"That's for sure," Gideon added.

The men continued to eat their breakfasts and carry on lighthearted conversations. The chance encounter had given all of them on opportunity to relieve the boredom of traveling.

Shad set his plate down and stretched his arms. "We've been chasing some outlaws all the way from Wichita Falls. Rumor has it they have a cabin on an inlet of the Arkansas River. If they're all still together, there are five of them. We could use some help and it wouldn't be much out of your way. If you help us take them, I'd wire you each a thousand dollars of the reward money when we get paid."

Gideon grinned skeptically. "So just like that we can make some money if we help you."

"Sure. Our odds go up considerably with your help. Donnie and I are honest. You have my word that I'd pay you. I offered you my food, didn't I?" Shad said in a defensive tone.

"That you did, but I think Finnie and I better worry about our own outlaws," Gideon said.

"We're all headed the same direction and the Arkansas River is about three hours from here. The cabin is supposed to be only an hour off the trail. You shouldn't lose over a half day," Shad pleaded.

"Shad, I've wasted a lot of time chasing down rumors that were plain wrong or where one hour away turned into five. I'm sorry," Gideon said.

Standing, Shad walked over to his saddlebags and pulled out wanted posters of the men he and Donnie were tracking. He handed them to Gideon.

"If money is not enough to make you help, maybe your sense of duty to the law will when you see what these men have done," Shad said.

Gideon held the posters so that he and Finnie could read them at the same time. Each member of the gang was wanted for murder, rape, robbery, and kidnapping.

"They are a bad lot," Finnie noted.

"That they are. I don't know if either of you have a wife or daughters, but no woman is safe around these pigs," Shad said.

Glancing at Finnie, Gideon saw the Irishman nod his head ever so slightly.

"All right, we'll help you. As persuasive as you are, you should be a politician."

Shad smiled before retrieving a pencil from his saddlebag and handing it to Gideon. "Write down your names and the bank where we're to wire the money on the back of one of the posters. I'm a man of my word."

After finishing breakfast, the four men began riding east. Finnie began regaling his new captive audience with tales of his boxing days, and had the two men roaring in laughter with his colorful descriptions. Gideon looked over at Finnie and shook his head, but kept his mouth shut. The deputy was still talking when the men reached the Arkansas River with the sun nearly straight up in the sky.

"If we're where I think we are, the cabin is supposed to be an hour north of here where a large creek feeds the river. The cabin sits a couple hundred yards up the creek," Shad said.

"Well, let's find out. I'd like to get this over with," Gideon said as he turned Buck.

Finnie stopped talking and began watching his surroundings as they rode. Gideon glanced over at his deputy as he suppressed a smile. Through all their days together in the war and now as lawmen, he could always count on the Irishman to be ready and accountable when the situation called for it.

They had ridden for just over an hour when they came upon a creek with deep banks. A grown over trail followed the creek to the northwest. "Everything looks as described," Shad said as he took the lead up the small path.

"I smell smoke," Finnie whispered after they had ridden a little ways.

"Maybe we should tie the horses here off the trail and walk the rest of the way," Shad suggested.

"So what's your plan?" Gideon asked.

"I figured you and Finnie can take the back and Donnie and I will take the front. They won't be going anywhere that way."

"But they could hole up in there for days if they've got supplies and water."

"I'll have a surprise for them if they try it," Shad said and winked.

Once the horses were tied out of sight of the trail, Shad again led the way. After walking a few hundred feet, the cabin came into view. The structure stood fifty yards from the creek under a canopy of large trees that blocked out direct sunlight. Smoke drifted lazily out of the chimney. Five horses stood tied under a lean-to, but nobody was outside of the cabin.

"Looks like we've found our men," Donnie whispered.

"I'll give you two time to work your way around to the back and then I'll call out to them. Be careful," Shad said.

Gideon and Finnie looped around the cabin. The land gently tapered uphill from the cabin and provided them an elevated position in which to take cover. Both of them took a position behind an oak large enough to conceal their bodies. The back side of the cabin had a door and two windows.

Finnie peeked around the tree and studied the cabin. "Damn, that cabin has four little gun ports in the logs. They look no bigger than six-inch squares. We'll never have a good shot."

Craning his head around the tree, Gideon had a look. "I knew this would be difficult. We're liable to be here for days. So much for catching our outlaws before they get to their homes."

"I wonder what surprise Shad was talking about."

"I have no idea. I think he was just making a joke."

From the front side of the cabin, Shad's voice boomed, "We have you surrounded. You can give up or die."

Shad's warning was answered with a round of gunshots. Gideon and Finnie poked their rifles around the side of the tree. Two of the gun ports had rifles sticking out of them. The two lawmen fired at the ports before retreating behind the tree. Two reciprocating shots thumped into the oaks.

"That's not much to shoot at," Finnie said.

"No, and our shooting downhill works against us in this situation," Gideon said.

For the next two hours, men inside of the cabin exchanged gunfire with the lawmen and bounty hunters. Finnie had managed to hit the barrel of a rifle held by an outlaw. The shot had knocked the gun downwards and sliding out of the gun port towards the ground before someone inside had yanked it back. Moments later a replacement rifle sent shots into the trees.

"That didn't accomplish much," Finnie remarked.

"I bet somebody has hands stinging like they grabbed a hornet's nest though."

"Not enough to keep him from shooting. We aren't getting anywhere," Finnie complained.

Gideon swung his rifle around the tree, but before he could draw a bead on the gun port, the bullet of a rifle took a chunk out of the tree above his head and sent bark showering down on his hat. "Damn, I just about had an extra hole in my head," he called out.

"I doubt a bullet would penetrate that German forehead of yours. I have this theory that you Germans have that prominent forehead to crack nuts," Finnie teased.

"I'd like to crack a pair of nuts right now."

The sound of someone's steps crunching through the woods towards them caused Gideon and Finnie to quit their jawing and train their rifles towards the noise.

"It's me," Shad called out as he maneuvered to a tree between Gideon and Finnie. He slid to the ground with his back against the trunk. "I wasn't expecting the cabin to be a fortress."

"Well, it is," Finnie said.

"Just keep taking a shot now and then so they know we're still here. I got some dynamite in my saddlebag.

After it gets dark, I'll slip in from the side and stick it in one of those gun ports, light it, and shove it inside the cabin. With all the tree cover, it should be damn dark. After the explosion, we'll see how much fight they have left in them," Shad said.

"Oh, Lordy. Have you ever handled that stuff before now?" Gideon asked.

"Yes, I have. I have enough that it should cause chaos," Shad said with a grin. "Aren't you glad you stopped for breakfast?"

"I'll be glad when this is over with," Gideon said.

"I'll do it on this side. They are manning three of the four holes on our side," Shad said as he peeked around the tree to have a look at the back side of the cabin. "Have they switched holes any?"

"Nah, they've stuck to the two middle ones," Finnie replied.

"All right, boys, see you later," Shad said before leaving.

For the rest of the day, Gideon and Finnie took turns firing an occasional shot at the cabin while Shad and Donnie did the same. The men hadn't eaten since breakfast and Finnie complained of hunger as his belly growled loudly.

As dusk settled in, Gideon had grown tired of the waiting and listening to Finnie complain. If he had it all to do over again, he'd never let them talk him into helping. He just wanted to get on Buck to ride towards Arkansas. "You know, if you hadn't been all fired up about eating breakfast with them, none of this would have happened. We could have gone on our merry way," he chided.

"Don't you start with me. I didn't see you refusing their food," Finnie said.

"Of course not, but if we hadn't of stopped, I would have had to listen to you bellyache all day."

"You're just irritable. Get over yourself."

Gideon gave up on the conversation and both men sat silently as the dark settled over them. The trees blocked out almost all of the light from the rising moon. They could barely see the unlit cabin from their position.

"The fun should start at any minute," Finnie said.

"Be careful. They might come out shooting," Gideon said to relieve his guilt for picking on Finnie.

"You do the same. I wouldn't want to miss out on your grumpy company," Finnie said with merriment in his voice.

A few minutes later, they saw a match glowing down by the cabin and then the sparks from the fuse before it disappeared from sight. Shad sounded like a herd of buffalo running as he sprinted away from the cabin. A moment later, the explosion obliterated the noise of his footsteps. Gideon stuck a finger in each ear and shook his hands as he winced in discomfort. Pieces of wood shingles could be heard hitting the ground as the material descended from flight. A fire burned around the hole blown through the roof and provided light to see the cabin. The wall that had endured the brunt of the explosion had logs bowing out and stood precariously.

The front door to the cabin opened a couple of minutes later. "We're coming out. Don't shoot," someone yelled.

Three men emerged from the cabin, dragging two of their partners with them. Shad and Donnie walked up to the outlaws with their rifles ready. The fugitives held their hands in the air and offered no resistance. All of them looked like roosters that had lost a cockfight. The two men on the ground had parts of their clothing burned off and the three men standing were covered in dirt and soot.

"Lie down on the ground," Shad ordered.

"We got them," Donnie bellowed for Gideon and Finnie to hear.

Shad checked the outlaws for weapons after Gideon and Finnie joined them. Two of the men were dead and the other three had all the fight knocked out of them. Finnie left to retrieve the horses, and when he returned, he tended to the injuries. The outlaw's ears were ringing so badly from the noise of the explosion that the Irishman had to yell at them in order for them to hear his questions. The injuries proved to be minor flash burns and a couple of puncture wounds from flying debris. Donnie bound the men with leather strips when Finnie had finished.

"Nothing to it," Shad joked.

"It worked. I'll give you that," Gideon said.

Flames began to engulf the cabin and the heat drove the men to a safe distance from the structure. Finnie and Donnie built a fire and began cooking salt pork while teasing each other on proper cooking techniques. By the time they fed the prisoners and themselves, the night seemed as if it had lasted for days. After binding the prisoners to trees, the men gladly turned in to get some sleep.

The next morning, Finnie awoke before anyone else and had a fire blazing by the time the others stirred from their sleep. Gideon, anxious to get back on the trail, prodded everyone into hurrying and insisted on a cold breakfast much to the Irishman's displeasure. By seven o'clock, all of the men were mounted up and the two bodies tied across their saddles. They headed out with the cabin still smoldering.

When they reached the main trail, Shad said, "I guess this is where we part."

"I'd say so and I've gained a new experience in capturing outlaws in the bargain," Gideon said as he reached over and shook the bounty hunter's hand.

"You'll have the money by the time you're back home if they don't piss around on paying the bounty. Either way, you have my word, it will be on its way."

"I believe you."

As the Texans rode away, Gideon and Finnie rode along the river looking for a place to cross.

"So do you think we'll get paid?" Finnie asked.

"I do. Either way, there are five less outlaws terrorizing the land. We did our part," Gideon said.

"Damn, I hate crossing rivers. I have a fear of drowning," Finnie said as he eased his horse into the water.

"I know you do. You've told me that at every river we've crossed since the first time we came upon one in the war," Gideon said as he walked Buck into the water.

"If I fall in, just stick your head in the water and drink the river down with that big mouth of yours."

Chapter 16

Doc walked in his slow shuffle down to the livery stable. His two oldest grandkids wanted to go horseback riding. Henry had once before ridden on the family's previous visit to Last Stand, but this would be Rose's first experience on a horse. The doctor explained to Blackie his need to rent a couple of gentle mounts and the blacksmith assured him that he had two old geldings that he kept for pleasure riding that would serve the purpose perfectly. Satisfied with Blackie's choices, Doc walked back to his office to await the arrival of his grandchildren.

Ethan had agreed to chaperone Henry and Rose, along with Benjamin and Winnie, on the ride. Sarah had graciously offered to keep all of the children for the night to give Doc some time to spend with John and Kate and to provide Sylvia an opportunity to play with Tad.

The three grandchildren arrived at the doctor's office without their parents accompanying them. Doc shepherded them down to the livery stable where Blackie had Doc's buggy waiting with the two geldings tied behind the rig. Rose began hopping around with excitement like a bunny rabbit and then cautiously approached one of the horses, rubbing its nose.

"It's so soft," Rose said in amazement.

"Watch out. It might bite you," Henry teased.

"I can tell that it likes me. I get to ride this black one."

Doc began swooping his arms to get his grandkids into the buggy as if he were shooing chickens. "The sooner we leave, the sooner you can be riding," he said.

With everyone crowded into the buggy, the doctor tapped the reigns to begin the journey to Ethan's ranch. Along the way, Doc divulged to his grandchildren some of the details of his life growing up in Pennsylvania as the son of a dry goods store owner. He then began reminiscing about moving to Boston to study medicine to become a doctor and of meeting the children's grandmother. Tad was too young to appreciate the recollections, but Henry and Rose listened attentively and asked questions much to the doctor's delight.

Winnie had already arrived at the Oakes cabin by the time Doc and his family pulled up into the yard. She, Benjamin, and Sylvia sat on the porch swing swaying wildly as they anxiously awaited the family's arrival.

"They're here," Benjamin bellowed to let his parents know of the arrival of their company.

Ethan and Sarah joined the children outside as Doc climbed out of the buggy and led his family up onto the porch. Winnie remained in awe of the slightly older Rose, finding it amazing that the big city girl actually liked her. She slid off the swing and sidled up next to Rose. Henry, still uncomfortable with his ascent into adulthood, stiffly shook Ethan's hand.

"Doc, as always, you've arrived just in time for a meal," Sarah teased.

"You don't know how this pains me, but I have to get back to have lunch with John and Kate. I know there will be no comparison to the taste of your food," Doc said.

"Well, I guess I'll try not to get my feelings hurt then."

Doc turned towards his grandkids. "You three make sure that you listen to Ethan and Sarah. Sarah can be meaner than a snake. Just ask poor Benjamin. You don't want to get on her bad side," he said and winked at Sarah.

By the time Doc returned to Last Stand, his belly growled and made him wish that he had stayed for lunch with the Oakes family. He was a little anxious about the meal with John and Kate anyway. They had seemed a little too eager to get him alone without the children, and he suspected that they had an agenda. He found both of them sitting in his office when he walked in.

"Did you get the kids all situated?" Kate asked.

"I did. Rose was so excited that I thought she would bust a seam. They'll have a fine time and the experience will be good for them," Doc replied.

"Let's go eat. I'm about starved," John said.

"Me and you, both. I gave up Sarah's cooking for you two. And you know how well Sarah can cook," Doc grumbled.

They walked down to Mary's Place where Charlotte seated them. The lunch crowd had already thinned down to one other table of diners, allowing Charlotte their near undivided attention.

"What'll you have, Doc? How about some old goat soup," Charlotte teased, causing John and Kate to burst out laughing.

Doc looked up from his menu as the joke slowly permeated his conscience. "Why are you teasing me? I thought you saved your wrath for Gideon and Finnie," he said earnestly.

"Well, they're both gone so that leaves you," Charlotte said with a smile so sweet looking as to mask all shades of the orneriness behind it.

The doctor stared at Charlotte a moment and scowled. "Little lady, you best remember that you might need my medical attention someday," he said. "Now bring me a beefsteak, corn, and a potato."

After taking John and Kate's orders, Charlotte practically skipped away from the table.

"She must like you," Kate said.

"I don't know about that. I think she just likes to be mean to everybody and pretend it's teasing," Doc said.

"I doubt that," John remarked.

As they waited for the food, they talked about Henry's plan to become a doctor and the possible futures of Rose and Tad. Kate began telling stories on her children that would have certainly embarrassed them in front of their grandfather and had him laughing so hard that he had to wipe his eyes.

Charlotte brought the food to the table, winking at Doc before leaving without flinging any more insults.

They had barely started eating their food when Kate said, "I sure hope the children are fine. I worry about Rose on a horse. It's a long ways to the ground. And Tad is liable to give Sarah fits. That child is a handful."

Doc swallowed a bite of food before speaking. "I'm sure they will be fine. Ethan will keep them on easy to ride trails. And don't worry about Sarah. I assure you that Tad has met his match if he thinks he can run roughshod with her. Child or not – nobody messes with Sarah," he said with a chuckle.

John nervously cleared his throat. "Father, we'd like to talk to you about you moving to Boston."

Doc looked up at his son. "I figured there was a reason you were so anxious to get together without the kids. Well, let's talk about it."

"We would move out here with you in a heartbeat if it were possible, but I have the bank to run. The board grumbled about me coming out here three years in a row as it is. It would make a lot more sense for you to retire and come live with us."

"The children adore you and you know I do, too," Kate added. "You might get to the point where you need somebody to help take care of you and you have no one here."

"I have several people that would see to me," Doc said defensively. "Mary, Sarah, and Abby would all look after me."

"I'm sure they would, but they have to look after their own families too. We're your family," Kate said.

"I know," Doc said. "But I'm not having any luck finding a new doctor and this town needs me."

John leaned forward. "Father, you've given your whole life to Last Stand. You don't owe it anything else."

Doc cut a piece of steak and chewed the bite methodically while he thought about what had been said. "It's a lot to contemplate. I surely would love to spend more time with all of you, but I just don't know."

Kate dropped her fork onto her plate, making a loud clank. "I can't fathom what you don't know. You and John have both suffered enough for the time that you were apart at his family's hands. You are not getting any younger and need to make up for as much lost time as possible. I think the answer is rather obvious."

Looking at the color that had come to his daughter-in-law's face, Doc couldn't help but smile. He had never before seen Kate angry. "I know you don't understand, but this place became my family after I gave up on ever seeing John all those years ago. That's a hard thing to turn my back on when I'm still needed here. I'm not saying yes or no right now. It's just a lot to think over."

Hoping to stymie his wife from saying anything else inflammatory, John said, "That's all we can ask, but know that all of us would love to have you live with us in Boston."

"Let's enjoy our meal. I never would have guessed that Charlotte's barrage would be the least of my worries," Doc said and chuckled.

Chapter 17

Stepping out onto the porch, Sarah scanned the yard for Sylvia. She had sent her outside to play after having had enough of her underfoot. The child had been restless and bored ever since the Hamilton family and Winnie had gone home after the horse ride and sleepover. Sarah rushed behind the cabin and still did not see her anywhere. She tried to keep herself from panicking. Ethan and Benjamin were gone checking the herd and she would have to find the little girl by herself. Thinking back, she assured herself that she had always been able to find Benjamin. He had disappeared into the thickets too many times to count. Calling out Sylvia's name, she began searching the woods. As she walked, Sarah chastised herself for not keeping a closer eye on the child. She should have seen this coming. For weeks now, Sylvia had been testing Ethan and her. Sylvia had already gone through so much in her young life that both of them had been reluctant to rein her in. Sarah knew that the lack of discipline had led to this.

While following the creek that Benjamin had always favored, Sarah called out again for Sylvia, but got no response. Along the creek bank, she found some tracks of the child and of their dog. Sarah walked and called out for another good five minutes with still no sighting of Sylvia. The footprints reassured her that she was following the right track, but she still worried that the child could drown in one of the natural pools along the creek. She shouted the child's name again and heard Red bark in response. As Sarah kept hollering, Red kept responding as she walked farther up the stream until she spotted the dog standing beside the little girl. Sylvia sat on the bank, playing in mud. Her hands were covered in the muck as well as her dress.

"Sylvia, what do you think you are doing?" Sarah asked sternly.

The little girl smiled up at Sarah as if nothing were out of the ordinary. "Red and I went for a walk."

Sarah looked down at the child, trying to decide what next to do. She wasn't sure whether Sylvia was trying to be charming or if the child had no idea that she had done anything wrong. Back in the day, Sarah would have dusted Benjamin's britches all the way back to the house. She wondered if she were getting soft in her old age or if she still feared being too rough on Sylvia, but she nixed the notion of a spanking either way. Instead, she swooped Sylvia off the ground and turned for home.

"Young lady, that was a bad thing that you did. You are never to leave the yard by yourself. A bear or a wolf could have eaten you," Sarah scolded in the harshest tone she had ever taken with the child.

Sylvia began sniffling. When Sarah's expression did not soften in the least, the situation deteriorated into all out bawling.

"I was looking for Heaven," Sylvia managed to say between sobs.

"Hush, I don't want to hear it," Sarah chided. "You won't find Heaven playing in the mud. I already told you that Heaven is in the sky. You can't walk to it and you can't go there until God calls you. If you think I'm mean, wait until a bear starts chewing off your fingers."

By the time they reached the cabin, Sylvia's crying hadn't subsided a lick, nor had Sarah's stern demeanor.

Sarah washed the child's hands and then roughly pulled the soiled dress off over Sylvia's head. She put the little girl in a nightgown and carried her to her bed.

"You are going to bed and you better not get out of it until I tell you that you can. Do you understand me?" Sarah demanded.

Sylvia's crying had slowed back to sniffling. She nodded her head. "Uh-huh. I'm sorry, Momma."

Sarah paused to study the child. Sylvia had never before called her momma. Up until now, the child had called her and Ethan by their names. As Sarah looked at Sylvia's snotty nose and red eyes, she doubted that the child was trying to play her to get back in her good graces. In fact, she wondered if Sylvia even realized what she had said.

"I know you are. Now don't forget what I told you," Sarah said before leaving the bedroom.

While walking into the kitchen, Sarah decided to start preparing supper. She began peeling and slicing potatoes, tossing them into a pan when finished. While she worked, she wondered if she had handled Sylvia's looking for Heaven properly. She knew that the child was still too young to understand about Heaven or death, but scaring Sylvia into never running off again had seemed like the most prudent thing to do. Come tomorrow, she'd talk to Sylvia about Heaven again. As she finished with the last spud, the front door opened, and she turned to see her husband and son walk into the cabin.

As Ethan hung his hat and gun belt on pegs by the door, he scanned the room. Usually Sylvia came running into his arms each night. "Where is Sylvia?" he asked.

"I sent her to bed. She went exploring today and I had to go find her," Sarah informed him.

"Oh, that's not good. You weren't too hard on her, were you?"

"No, I wasn't too hard on her. Goodness, I didn't know that you thought I was capable of being cruel," Sarah said, placing her hands on her hips.

"I didn't mean that. It's just that we've gone kind of easy on her up to now."

"That's right, we have, and it's time to stop. Enough time has gone by since the fire and it's time to start raising her just as we did Benjamin. We're liable to have an outlaw on our hands if we don't."

Ethan looked at his wife and tried to figure out where the conversation might be headed. It seemed to him that Sarah was sending out mixed signals. She seemed awfully perturbed with Sylvia considering that Sarah had fetched Benjamin more times than he could remember. He hated it when he had to decipher in between the lines of what Sarah was saying. Usually, he got it wrong.

"Are you having second thoughts about us raising her?" Ethan asked.

"Ethan Oakes," Sarah called out, her voice loud and shrill. "For a preacher, sometimes you are the most clueless man I've ever known when it comes to understanding people. What have I ever said or done that would make you think I would give up on Sylvia. You must secretly think that you're married to a witch. I love that child just like she's my own. I've gotten mad at you and Benjamin more times in one day than I have that child the whole time that she has been here and I never wanted to get rid of either of you. Honestly,

Ethan, sometimes you appall me. I have to go to the smokehouse and get a pork shoulder."

As soon as Sarah walked outside, Benjamin grinned mischievously at his father.

"Why are you smiling?" Ethan asked.

"She sure got you. You better reach back and see if you still have a backside. Even I know enough not to ask a question like that. Nobody questions Momma's love for us," Benjamin said.

"Oh, shut up or I'm liable to tell on you for something that you did that I hid from your mother to keep you from getting a licking."

Sarah walked back in carrying the pork. She stopped in front of Ethan. "I still can't believe that you thought I might want to give her back," she said with exasperation.

"Sarah, I'm sorry. You just seemed so upset over this that I wasn't sure what you were getting at," Ethan said defensively.

"I was upset. She scared me. Anything could have happened to her out there. I don't want her growing up thinking she can do as she pleases."

"Well, I don't think she'll start robbing banks tomorrow."

Peering at Ethan, Sarah couldn't help but laugh. "You're right, but we have to start making her mind. I can hardly wait until the judge comes to town and makes the adoption official. Go on and get her out of bed. Just have a little talk with her. You can be the nice parent this time."

"Are you sure you don't want me to beat her first?" Ethan asked sarcastically.

"You could get back on my bad side real quick. Sylvia did call me momma today," Sarah said proudly.

"She might have called you momma, but I bet she was thinking something else," Ethan said before disappearing into the bedroom.

Chapter 18

Cyrus Capello's lawyer arrived at the Last Stand jail a week before the trial was set to begin just as his telegram had promised. The attorney was well known in the legal community of Denver and had gotten Cyrus out of a scrape once before years ago.

The lawyer marched up to the sheriff's desk and said, "My name is Rutherford Ellis, Esquire and I'm Mr. Capello's lawyer. I need to consult with my client immediately."

Zack looked up from the desk trying to suppress his amusement upon seeing the dress of the dandy. The lawyer stood before him in loud stripe pants, a velvet vest, and a coat with tails. Completing his ensemble was a tall top hat perched upon his head. Zack stood up and walked around the desk. "I need to check you for weapons," he said.

"I'm not accustomed to such proceedings. I'm a respected lawyer," Rutherford protested as he held out his arms.

"Well, I'm not accustomed to trusting anyone associated with Cyrus Capello. Trust and Cyrus do not exactly go hand in hand," Zack said as he patted down the lawyer. "Come with me."

As Zack grabbed the keys to the cells, he led the attorney into the cell room and unlocked Cyrus's door. "You have a visitor," he said before he locked Rutherford in with Cyrus. On his way out, he shut the door to the cell room to give the men some privacy.

"It's about time you showed up," Cyrus said as a way of greeting.

"I am not in the habit of leaving the comforts of Denver for these little worthless mountain towns. Be thankful you have the money to afford me. This is costing you a bundle," Rutherford said.

Sneering, Cyrus said, "That's what I like about you lawyers. You're just like me – money above all else."

Rutherford checked to make sure the door was shut. "Tell me the situation," he ordered.

Cyrus recounted all that had transpired since the night that Andrew Moss had been murdered. Rutherford scribbled notes furiously as the saloonkeeper talked. Once Cyrus finished talking, he pulled a cigar from his breast pocket, bit off the cap, and lighted his stogie.

"Which one of you actually killed Mr. Moss?" Rutherford asked.

"I gave a little nod and Jimmy slipped behind him to slit his throat. Damned near cut off his head," Cyrus said with a touch of amusement.

"You have yourself in a most dire situation, Cyrus."

"Can't you put all the blame on Jimmy and make me out to be an innocent bystander."

"I think that the most we can hope for is to create enough doubt that the judge decides not to hang you. You're looking at a long prison sentence at best."

"What? I'm paying you all that money and that's your solution. She is a whore after all. Surely you can discredit her," Cyrus yelled.

"Possibly, but you have to keep in mind that your reputation is far from stellar, too. I'm sure the district attorney will do his homework," Rutherford said.

"Lawyers are the ones that should be hanged," Cyrus shouted.

"Cyrus, calm yourself. I didn't put you in this situation. With your past, I would have thought that you would be smart enough not to murder a whore's old beau right in front of her. You have not given me much in which to work with."

"Get out of here. My saloon is down the street to the east. Get your ass down there and tell Spenser to get his ass down here. I think he's avoiding me and that's not wise if he knows what's good for him," Cyrus said as he stood and began pacing.

Rutherford grabbed the lapels of his jacket and stuck out his chest. "I am not in the habit of running errands. I am a lawyer after all."

"I don't give a damn what you are. If you want to get paid, you'll do exactly as you are told. I wouldn't push me if I were you. I can't see where I'm getting much use out of you as it is," Cyrus said as he stopped inches from the lawyers face.

The lawyer seemed to melt under the saloonkeeper's glare. "Very well."

Cyrus bellowed for Zack and the deputy came to get the lawyer. Rutherford Ellis walked out of the jail without bothering to say another word. He promptly located the Pearl West and found Spenser tending bar. The attorney, still smarting from the ire of Cyrus, told the bartender in no uncertain terms that his presence was demanded immediately at the jail.

Spenser, already nervous for avoiding Cyrus, made a beeline to the jail. Zack patted him down and led him to the cell room.

"You're mighty popular today. I'm betting the next visitor brings you cake," Zack said as he let Spenser into the cell.

"Screw you," Cyrus barked.

"Oh, Cyrus, you forget who brings you your food," Zack said before leaving.

"Where in the hell have you been?" Cyrus demanded.

"Running your saloon. There's really nothing much to tell you," Spenser said.

"Did Oliver make it into town?"

"He's been here a few days."

"And you didn't think I needed to know that?" Cyrus inquired.

"He hasn't found the whore yet. He spent a day watching that deputy's cabin and a day watching the sheriff's place and saw no sign of her. I even had him watch Ethan Oakes' ranch. I thought that maybe they had her there since he's a friend of the sheriff. Zack has her hid good," Spenser said.

Cyrus kicked the bed frame and hurt his foot in the process. He swore as he hopped around the room on one foot while holding the other. When the pain subsided, he grabbed Spenser by the shirt and pulled the bartender so close to his face that he could smell the garlic on his breath. "Jimmy was the only one I could ever count on to do things right most of the time. Of course, he's the one that got me into this predicament by not cleaning up the mess. The rest of you are a bunch of imbeciles. Do you realize that if they hang me or throw me in prison that you'll be out of a job? You tell Oliver to follow Zack wherever he goes no matter if it's just to take a piss and make sure he doesn't get spotted. Zack will check on the whore. We only have a week. Do you understand?"

Spenser nodded so rapidly that he looked as if his head were on a spring.

"Good. Now get out of here and get to work," Cyrus yelled, sending spittle into Spenser's face.

On hearing the shouting, Zack checked to see what was going on in the cell. Spenser rushed to the door and told the deputy he was ready to leave. Zack let him out of the cell and escorted Spenser to the front of the jail.

"That Cyrus is a peach to work for, isn't he?" Zack asked as he sat down in his chair.

"You have no idea. Be glad you're a deputy. A bullet couldn't be worse than dealing with Cyrus," Spenser said before walking out the door.

Back at the saloon, Spenser pounded on the door to Oliver Townes' room until the hired killer let him in. After Spenser ran one of the whores out of the room, he delivered Cyrus's instructions. Oliver took to the orders just as the bartender figured he would. He cursed up a storm and threatened to ride out of town on the spot. As Spenser watched Oliver rant and rave, he reminded himself that the other couple of times that Cyrus had hired Oliver in the past, they had also been challenges unto themselves. In the end, the killer had always made the problems disappear.

Finally, Spenser had enough of shenanigans. He didn't really fear Oliver anyway. The killer was short and spindly, and the bartender thought he could take him in a fight. "That's enough," he yelled. "Either do your job or get on your damn horse and leave. You're not the only one that can do the job."

Oliver gave him the evil eye, but shut up. He grabbed his gun belt and walked out of the room. After clomping loudly down the stairs, he went behind the bar and grabbed a bottle of whiskey and a glass. He then took a seat at a table by a window in the front of the saloon where he could keep an eye on the jail. Oliver pulled the cork from the bottle with his teeth and poured three fingers worth of whiskey into the glass. His first sip of the day gave him some respite from the loud bartender.

By the time that five o'clock rolled around, Oliver felt flushed and mellowed out from the whiskey. He would have liked to grab one of the whores and take her to his room, but thought better of it. Locked up or not, Cyrus Capello was not a man to be trifled with. He watched through the window as Zack exited the jail and mounted his horse. Oliver drained the last of the whiskey from his glass and walked out of the saloon to climb onto his mount.

During the war, Oliver had been an advance scout for the Confederacy. The one thing that job had taught him how to do well above all others was the ability to travel stealthily. He followed Zack at a good distance as the deputy traveled south out of town. The lawman would stop occasionally and look back over his shoulder, but Oliver never provided an opportunity for Zack to spot him. After Zack rode for over a mile out of town, he turned and headed northwest. Oliver pulled his horse to a stop and grinned. He knew the deputy would soon lead him to the whore. Before the night was through, he'd kill Fancy and be back at the saloon with money, whiskey, and his pick of the Pearl West whores.

Oliver followed Zack around the sheriff's cabin that the hired killer had already watched for a whole day.

After crossing some grazing land, the deputy headed into rougher territory covered in timber, brush, and some rock. From Oliver's years of scouting, he had a hunch that he was close to the location of the whore. He hid his horse behind an outcrop of stone and continued on foot. His first sign that Fancy was near came on the breeze with the smell of smoke. A few minutes later, he heard Zack calling out to the whore.

String Callow came out of the cabin and greeted Zack.

"I thought I'd check on Fancy. I have some news for her," Zack said.

"Come on in. She's fixing supper," String said and held the door open for the deputy to enter.

"Hi, Fancy. How are you doing?" Zack asked.

"If you like living with shy cowboys that don't talk much, well, then I'm wonderful," Fancy said sarcastically.

Zack wasn't sure if the whore was kidding or actually complaining about her living companion, but he didn't intend to find out the answer. "I wanted to let you know that the judge is arriving next week. On the morning of the day that you're set to testify, I'll show up here early and get you to town. Once you give your testimony, you'll be able to do as you please."

"Thank God. I'm about bored out of my mind," Fancy said as she stared at String.

The cowboy averted his eyes from the whore's glare and didn't speak.

"Well, you may be bored, but it looks like you are doing just fine. Being out here in the middle of nowhere sure beats being dead in town," Zack said in defense of String.

"That it does. And I do appreciate what you and String have done for me, but I'm a city girl that likes the action."

Once again, Zack didn't want to know the answer to whatever action Fancy felt might be missing from her life. "I need to be getting home. If you start to get stir crazy, just remember that it's about over with."

By the time Zack walked out the door, Oliver had concealed himself amongst some rocks and had a view of the cabin. He watched the deputy ride away and smiled with satisfaction. All he had to do now was wait for nightfall. This murder would be as easy as taking candy from a baby.

As darkness settled over the land, Oliver had to listen to his belly growl. The glow of the whiskey had worn off long ago and the hours of lying on a bed of hard rock had made him stiff. His good mood had faded with the light. He got to his feet and maneuvered into the shadows of the cabin. Out of habit, he worked his knife up and down in its sheath a couple of times, figuring the wait would soon be over. One of the two people in the cabin was bound to come outside for a nature call before long.

String walked outside and over to the edge of the small yard. Oliver couldn't believe the height of the man. He guessed the cowboy stood a good six feet and six or seven inches. The height also presented a problem for slitting the throat. Oliver doubted he could reach over the man's shoulder and wield his knife successfully across the cowboy's throat. After sheathing his knife, the hired killer pulled his gun out of the holster and began stalking String. He didn't want to shoot the gun and alert Fancy. Whores tended to know how to defend themselves and he'd come across plenty that were pretty fair shots. As he neared String, he could hear the cowboy humming as his piss splattered on the ground. Oliver swung the gun as hard as he could and crashed the barrel into the back of the cowboy's head. String swayed for a moment like a tall tree in a windstorm and then collapsed in a heap upon the ground. While holstering his gun, Oliver let out a little giggle at the thought of the cowboy's pecker hanging out of his trousers in the dirt.

Fancy never even looked up when Oliver walked into the cabin. She was busy writing a letter by lamplight.

"Hello, Fancy. It's been a long time. The last time I got a poke out of you was in Denver when Cyrus needed my services," Oliver said with a leer.

As Fancy jumped to her feet, she knocked over her chair and backed into the corner. The look of sheer terror on the whore's face made all the waiting worth the effort for the killer and aroused him.

"String is outside. You better get out of here," Fancy screamed.

"I bashed the brains out of your cowboy," Oliver said as he drew his knife.

"Leave me alone," she cried out.

"Fancy, we both know I can't do that. I sure do love me a good fiery redhead though. Give me a good poke and I'll make dying nice and quick. You fight me and I'm just liable to make a sport out of killing you," he said as he approached her.

Fancy tried to dash past Oliver, but he grabbed her arm and slung her down on the bed, landing on top of her with all his weight. Oliver pushed the point of the knife against Fancy's neck as she started to whimper, and kissed her hard on the mouth to try to drown out the sounds and to dominate her.

"Fancy, you should have known to never go up against Cyrus. That's a losing battle," Oliver said as he tore at her garments. "Now be good."

Closing her eyes, Fancy began screaming hysterically as Oliver ripped away her clothing.

The screaming stirred String from his unconsciousness. He managed to get into a sitting position and shove his member back into his pants. As he tried to figure out what had happened, all he knew for certain was that his head hurt unmercifully and his vision was blurred. The screaming slowly permeated his conscience and he realized that Fancy was in trouble. He got to his feet and swayed like a drunkard as he stumbled towards the cabin. A sense of urgency propelled him up the stairs and into the shack. All of the screaming made String squint in pain as he saw the man raping Fancy on his bed. He pulled his revolver out of the holster hanging on the wall and staggered towards the bed. Neither Fancy nor the man saw him approach. String reached down with his left hand and grabbed the little man by the back of his coat collar. He took a deep breath to steady himself and slung the man with all his might. Oliver flew through the air as if he had suddenly gained wings. The hired killer's back crashed against the wall and he slid to the floor. String raised his Colt and started shooting. He kept firing well after Oliver had died and continued cocking the gun and squeezing the trigger as the hammer clicked against empty rounds.

Fancy managed to calm herself enough to stand up on the bed in near total nakedness so that she could easily reach String. She gently placed a hand around his forearm, and with the other, she grasped the gun. "You can stop. You've killed him," she said.

String let her take the gun from him. He turned and looked at her blankly. "I don't know what happened. I'm sorry."

"You don't have any reason to be sorry. He hit you in the skull. You're hurt and the back of your head is bleeding. Now sit down in the chair and let me have a look at you."

"I've never before shot anybody," String said absentmindedly.

Fancy led String to the chair and grabbed a towel. Focusing on his injury made it easier not to think about what she had just been through. She had been raped before, but had never been moments away from dying. That was something she didn't want to contemplate right now. She dabbed at the blood on the back of his head. "You have a big goose egg back here. I knew that hard head of yours would prove good for something. It's about stopped bleeding and I don't know what else to do. String, you saved my life."

As String bent his head down, he cupped his face in his hands. He tried to force his mind to clear, but he felt as if he were in a fog. Fancy sat down in front of him, and he looked up at her, but still couldn't quite get a handle on what had just transpired. "You need to get on some clothes," he said in a voice that sounded drunk.

"Honey, I've spent half my life naked in front of men. Never had any complain before tonight. I want to make sure that you're all right and maybe the view will help clear your head," she teased.

String managed to actually smile. The bashing of his brain seemed to have knocked out his self-consciousness around women for once. "Maybe," he said.

Fancy reached over and gently took String by the chin. "I've been so mean to you and now you go and save me from certain death. String, thank you," she said as tears began to well up in her eyes.

Chapter 19

Waking up from the throbbing in his head, String opened his eyes to find Fancy curled up asleep against him. He jumped at the sight, causing him to grimace with even more pain. The sudden movement didn't awaken Fancy, but she did throw her leg over the top of his. Looking at her again, he felt relieved to see that she wore a nightgown. He distinctly remembered seeing her naked. As he lay there, the memory of the previous night slowly came back to him. His mind no longer felt as if it were in a fog as he pieced the events together. He realized that the man that he killed must have followed Zack to the cabin.

"Fancy, wake up. We have things to do," String called out gently.

The whore opened her eyes and gazed up at the cowboy. "How are you feeling?" she asked.

"My mind is working just fine, but my head feels like I got kicked by a mule."

"Poor thing. You're my hero," she said and stretched her neck to give String a kiss on the cheek.

String turned a bright shade of pink. "We need to get moving," he mumbled.

"I don't know. This feels pretty good to me. Don't you like snuggling with a woman?"

The pink color in String's face turned to red and spread to his ears. "Zack needs to know that he was followed."

"You've never had a woman before, have you? I'll say this once and never mention it again – cowboy, I could make a pretty fair man out of you if you'd let me. There are a lot worse things in the world than settling down with a retired whore. I hear that Mary used to be one, and her and Finnie sure seem happy," she said as she climbed out of bed. She no longer saw the need for modesty around String and slipped her nightgown off right in front of him.

String got out of bed and turned his back to Fancy, hiding his arousal as he pulled on his trousers over his long underwear. He grabbed his shirt and had it all the way buttoned before he turned around and felt relieved to see that she was dressed.

"I'll fix us some breakfast," Fancy said as she grabbed some kindling.

"I'll go saddle my horse. I'm going to have to drag the body out of here to Abby's place. I can use her wagon to take him to town," String said as he strapped on his holster.

Sting walked outside and saw the body that he had dragged into the yard. He felt sheepish about the six bullet holes he counted in the man's shirt, but banished the notion with the thought that too many were better than not enough. After saddling his horse, he retrieved his lariat and tied the rope around the dead man's feet.

Fancy stuck her head out the door. "Breakfast is ready," she said before quickly disappearing back inside the cabin.

As they sat at the little table eating eggs and bacon, String watched Fancy while she ate. She seemed happier and more lighthearted than she had on any day since she came to the cabin. He couldn't understand how she could appear so carefree.

After String finally worked up his nerve, he said, "I know last night had to be scary. Are you all right?"

Fancy gave him a little smile. "Last night after you fell asleep, I sat here thinking about what happened. I decided that I could feel sorry for myself because that swine raped me and was about ready to slit my throat or I could feel blessed that a gangly awkward cowboy saved my life. I chose the second."

String could feel himself turning pink again. "You were worth the headache," he said and then laughed after realizing his double entendre.

"I plan to be," Fancy said and winked.

Glancing down at his plate, String concentrated on his food and didn't speak again until he had finished his meal. "You should be safe here. I'm just sure that man followed Zack and nobody else knows where you are. I need to go," he said.

"I don't want to be alone. Take me with you," Fancy pleaded.

"But I'm going to town. People will see you."

"I'd feel safer in town with you by my side than I would out here all alone."

String let out a sigh, knowing he'd lost the battle. "All right, let's go."

After climbing into the saddle, String kicked his boot out of the stirrup so that Fancy could put her foot in it as he pulled her up behind the cantle. He wasn't sure if she was scared of horses, but she sure squeezed him tightly around the waist as they headed out dragging the body down the trail. Before they reached Abby's cabin, String untied the lariat from the saddle horn and left the body, fearing the children would be out in the yard.

Abby sat on the porch waiting for her ranch hand. She planned to give him hell for being late until she looked out and saw him riding up with Fancy. Thinking better of it, she asked, "What's going on?"

String told her all that had happened and his plan to take the body to town in her buckboard.

"Bless both of your hearts," Abby said. "There's a tarp in the barn you can use to cover the body."

"Much obliged. I'm sorry for the inconvenience," String said.

Abby waved her hand through the air at the suggestion. "Fancy, why don't you stay here with me? We'll be safe here together and I'm sure that Zack would prefer you to stay out of sight. That boy has his hands full as it is."

Fancy was reluctant to let go of String, but decided that Abby was right. It had been forever since she had spent time with a real lady and the notion appealed to her. "All right," she said. String took her by the arm and helped her slide down off the horse.

String rode to the barn and hitched the buckboard up to a horse before heading out to get the body. A pain shot through his head as he squatted to lift the man, but overall his headache felt much better than when he had awakened that morning. After covering Oliver with the tarp, he started for town.

Nobody paid the ranch hand any attention as he rode through Last Stand. He had worried the whole trip that Zack wouldn't be at the jail, but felt relieved to see his horse tied out front.

Walking into the jail, String said, "I need you to see something out here."

Surprised to see String in town, Zack put on his hat and followed the cowboy outside.

String pulled the tarp back enough to show Oliver's head. "I'm pretty sure he followed you to the cabin," he said before recounting once again the events of the previous night.

Zack pulled off his hat and rubbed his forehead. His legs felt weak from guilt and the feeling of failure. "I'm so sorry. I promise you that I kept an eye out. I can't believe he followed me without me seeing him."

"Don't blame yourself. You didn't start this mess," String said.

"Go over and let Doc check your head. Don't come out until I come get you," Zack said as he looked around to see if anybody was watching.

String ambled across the street and disappeared inside the doctor's office. Zack marched into the jail and back into the cell room.

"Stand up and put your back to the bars. I've got something to show you," Zack ordered.

Cyrus seemed taken aback by the command, but did as he was told. After cuffing the saloonkeeper, Zack walked Cyrus out to the wagon and pulled the tarp off the body.

"Do you know him?" Zack asked.

"Never seen him before," Cyrus answered a little too quickly.

Zack watched as the color drained from Cyrus's face.

"You're such a damn liar. I bet you just felt that noose getting a little tighter around your neck," Zack said before shoving Cyrus towards the jail.

Once he had Cyrus locked back in the cell, Zack took the wagon to the undertaker and deposited the body.

He then parked the wagon in front of Doc's office and went inside the building.

"How is he?" Zack asked the doctor.

"He'll live. It's a good thing he has a hard head. He's lucky his skull isn't fractured. I gave him a tincture of willow bark for the pain," Doc replied.

"Do you think Fancy will be all right?" Zack asked String.

"I think so. She's seems to be more thankful that she's alive than bothered by what happened."

"Well, go on home and take it easy. I'm truly sorry to bring this upon you."

"We'll be fine. You need to be careful. Cyrus seems to be a desperate man," String said as he got to his feet.

After the cowboy left, Doc said, "He's right, you know. You need to be careful. This might not be over with yet."

"I sure wish Gideon were here. He would have never let somebody follow him like that. Doc, I'm in over my head," Zack lamented.

"Last time I checked, Gideon didn't walk on water. He's made plenty of mistakes. I think he'll be real proud of how you've handled things."

"I sure hope so. I had better get back to the jail before Cyrus tries something else. See you later," Zack said as he walked out the door.

Back at the jail, Zack sat at the desk and relived every moment of the journey to String's cabin. He still couldn't fathom how he had been followed and never managed to spot his tracker. Not only did he feel consumed with guilt for what String and Fancy had gone through, but embarrassed for such a complete failure of his job. Zack despised failing at anything.

He'd been that way since childhood and he desperately wished that he could relive the previous day.

Spenser walked into the jail from the Pearl West. "I need to see Cyrus," he stated.

"You were just here yesterday," Zack said irritably.

"I've never run a saloon before now. There's a lot that I don't know and have to ask Cyrus."

Zack patted down Spenser before grabbing the keys off the desk. He led the visitor back to the cell room and left him with Cyrus. "Be quick," he said as he left the room and shut the door.

"Oliver followed the deputy yesterday evening and never came back. I don't know what to make of it," Spenser said.

Cyrus gave the bartender a disgusted look. "Oliver is dead. Zack made a point of showing him to me laid out in the back of a wagon."

"Did he kill him?"

"I don't know who killed him. The point is that he's dead and Fancy isn't," Cyrus barked.

Dropping down onto the bed, Spenser asked, "What do we do now?"

"You're going to have to break me out of here. I'm not sitting around to go to prison or get hanged."

"I'm not a criminal. I'm a bartender," Spenser protested.

"I'll pay you three thousand dollars. I have a safe full of cash. You can go anywhere you want with that kind of money and start a new life."

With his interest piqued, Spenser asked, "How would I do it?"

"Does the blacksmith know you?"

"I don't think so. He never comes into the saloon," Spenser answered.

"Good. Change your clothes so you don't look like a bartender and go buy two good horses. Tie them in the alley behind the Pearl West. Tonight is Zack's night to stay at the jail. He turns the lights out around ten. I have a loaded shotgun in the corner of my office. Barge in here a little before ten. Don't shoot him unless you have no choice. That shotgun will wake up the whole town. I'll get the money out of the safe and then we'll ride. I know where we can hide," Cyrus said.

"Cyrus, how do I know I can trust you?"

"Listen, I may be a lot of things, but I'm not about to kill you after you save me from the noose. I love money, but I love my neck more. That's a small price to pay for freedom," Cyrus said and offered his hand.

The two men shook hands before Spenser hailed Zack and left the jail.

As the time neared noon, Zack walked to the doctor's office and asked Doc if he'd like to go to lunch with him. The two men wandered down to the Last Chance and took seats at a table. Mary stood tending bar when they walked into the saloon. She prided herself in her ability to read the mood of men and Zack's demeanor had trouble written all over it. Delta brought the men plates of food and Mary carried over two beers. She set them down and took a seat.

"What's wrong with you?" she asked Zack.

Zack explained what had happened.

"I think you should look at the bright side of things. It could have been a lot worse. The only people that don't make mistakes are the ones that don't do a darn thing," Mary offered.

"I doubt Gideon will think so, and I doubt he or Finnie would have made the same mistake," Zack said dejectedly.

"Oh, stop. You've done a fine job under trying circumstances. Gideon and Finnie were schooled in war. They have a lot more experience in this kind of thing than you do and who's to say they wouldn't have done the same thing. Quit being so hard on yourself."

"I told him basically the same thing," Doc chimed in.

"I'll sure be glad when they get back. Joann hates staying in the cabin by herself. Our life would be back to normal if not for me having to play deputy," Zack complained.

"Gideon will be proud of you and the town owes you its appreciation. We'd have bedlam right now if not for you," Mary said.

Zack managed a small smile. "I suppose," he said before taking a drink of beer.

"Just think, the trial will be next week, and once that's finished, things should get back to normal," she said.

"I don't think they'll be normal until Cyrus is hanged or sent off to prison," Zack said.

"Just take it a day at a time and you'll be fine," Mary said.

"How's Sam?" Doc asked.

"He's fine. He misses his daddy. Zack's not the only one that'll be glad when those two get home. Where's your family?"

"They are shopping today. They've fell in love with ranch clothing and you can't find that stuff in Boston," Doc said.

"The time is getting close for them to go home, isn't it? What are you going to do?" Mary asked.

Doc took a drink of beer and sighed as he set the mug down on the table. "I don't have a clue. They really want me to go back to Boston with them, and God knows I love spending time with the family, but I don't know if I can leave Last Stand. I've spent my whole adult life here and I don't know what the town would do without a doctor."

Mary blew out her breath. "I don't know what to say, but that I feel for you. That's a hard choice and I'm certainly not an impartial bystander. I do want you to be happy though. Do what's best for you. I better get back to work," she said before returning to the bar.

Zack spent the rest of the day taking walks of the town and talking to merchants to pass the time. At Mayor Hiram Howard's general store, he bought a copy of *Tom Sawyer*. He hadn't read a book in years, but he had heard Benjamin mention numerous times how funny the story was and decided to give it a try. Doc had plans with his family so Zack ate supper alone at Mary's Place. Charlotte took pity on him and sat down at his table to talk between serving orders of food without dishing out any of her usual sarcasm.

Afterward, he brought Cyrus a plate of food before sitting down at the desk. He turned up the wick on the oil lamp and opened *Tom Sawyer*. At first, he struggled with the literary dialect spellings, but once he got the hang of it, he found himself engrossed in the story and laughing aloud as the night passed.

∞

Doc dined with his family in the hotel dining room. Once they finished the meal, the group crowded into one of the family's hotel rooms and began playing the board game *The Checkered Game of Life*. The adults sipped on brandy as they played and Kate had even relented in pouring Rose a small portion of the liquor. As the night progressed, the laughter and merriment grew louder until a hotel clerk knocked on the door and informed the family that guests wishing to retire for the evening had complained.

The complaint caused Doc to say his goodbyes. He strolled out of the hotel and headed for his office. The brandy had him feeling flush and a tad giddy. He hadn't played a game other than cards in years and he cherished the time spent with the family. The evening had been magnificent and he paused to pull a stogie from his pocket and light it. As he puffed on the cigar to get it burning evenly, he swore he saw somebody dash into the jail.

Doc had caught a glimpse of Spenser barreling into the jail with the shotgun butt braced against his hip and pointed at the deputy. Zack looked up still grinning from a passage he'd read in *Tom Sawyer*.

"Deputy, please don't make me hurt you. Now stand up and take your gun belt off slowly and set it on the desk," Spenser ordered as he cocked a barrel of the gun.

Zack stood slowly and did as instructed. He raised his hands into the air without being told to do so. "Just take it easy. I don't want to die."

"Grab the keys and go unlock Cyrus," Spenser demanded.

Gently picking up the keys, Zack walked slowly to the cell room and unlocked the cell.

"Back away from the door," Cyrus yelled.

Doing as he was told, Zack retreated farther into the room. Cyrus exited the cell and joined Spenser.

"Now get in the cell and stand facing the corner farthest from the door," Cyrus ordered.

As soon as Zack complied, Cyrus ran to the door and locked it.

"You can turn around. I have something to say to you," Cyrus said and waited for Zack to face him. "You're one lucky son of a bitch because I would love to kill your smug ass. I'll be honest with you though – I fear that damn father-in-law of yours. I truly believe he would follow me into the bowels of hell if I killed you and I'm sure he'd make sure I died a tortuous death. So thank your daddy-in-law the next time you see him for keeping you alive," Cyrus said before dashing out of the cell room and slamming the door shut.

Cyrus stopped at the desk and dropped the keys before strapping on Zack's holster. "Are the horses waiting?" he asked.

"Just like you asked," Spenser replied.

"I hope I never see this town again. Let's get the hell out of here," Cyrus said as they moved towards the door.

The two men stepped out onto the boardwalk and looked around. Doc was crossing the street toward them with his shotgun.

As Doc recognized Cyrus by the light of the streetlamp, he yelled, "You two don't move."

"You old son of a bitch. You're the one that kept me from killing that damn whore in the first place," Cyrus yelled as he drew Zack's gun.

Cyrus fired at the same time that Doc discharged both barrels of his shotgun. The roar of the guns echoed up and down the street loudly enough to wake the dead. Doc spun around from the force of the bullet turning him and fell facedown onto the street. The blast of buckshot lifted Cyrus and Spenser off their feet and slammed them into the side of the jail. Both were dead by the time they slid to the ground.

The Last Chance and Pearl West emptied of patrons and employees as everyone ran into the street to see what all the commotion was. Mary saw the body sprawled in the street and began running. Before she even got to the body, a foreboding that it was Doc came upon her. She reached him before anyone else and flipped over the doctor. Doc opened his eyes and blinked a couple of times.

"Oh, Doc, how badly are you hurt?' Mary cried out as she sat down on the road and cradled the doctor's head.

"I don't know. My whole left side is numb," Doc said.

Mary brushed the dirt away from Doc's mouth. "Help is here," she said as she began rocking her body and sobbing. "Don't you dare leave me. You're my rock and you promised me that you'd be here for Sam."

"I'm too cantankerous to die," Doc said meekly.

"What were you thinking? You're getting a little old for stopping jail escapes," Mary said as she looked at the two bodies against the jail.

"And miss out on getting cradled in the arms of a pretty lady? Go check on Zack. Cyrus tried to escape," Doc said through clenched teeth.

"I'm not going anywhere," she said as she spotted the wound at the top of his left arm.

"Send somebody then," Doc said and winced. "The numbness is leaving and pain is coming."

Looking up at the gathering crowd, Mary yelled, "Somebody go in the jail and check on Zack."

Blackie had run from the livery stable and stood by Mary trying to catch his breath. "I'll go," he said.

After Blackie maneuvered through all the people surrounding the bodies, he had to drag Cyrus away from the door to get inside of the jail. He and Zack emerged from inside moments later.

"Oh, Doc, what have I done?" Zack asked as he knelt beside the doctor.

"Help me to my feet. Let's get inside my office and see how bad it is," Doc said.

"Don't you want us to carry you?"

"No, I do not. Now let's go," Doc ordered.

Blackie and Zack lifted the doctor to his feet, causing him to curse in pain. Doc swayed unsteadily as they walked him into his office. Mary grabbed a pair of scissors and began cutting the sleeves of his coat and shirt on his left arm. The material dropped away revealing a chunk of meat blown away just below the shoulder joint of his arm.

Doc looked at his wound. "That's not so bad. I thought the injury was worse than it is and had hit my shoulder joint."

"What do you want me to do?" Mary asked as she started crying again.

"Somebody better go get my family. I imagine they'd be upset if they didn't find out until morning. Henry can clean and bandage my arm. That's all that can be done anyway. Make sure you tell them that I'll be fine," Doc said.

"I'll go," Blackie volunteered.

Zack began pacing the room. "Doc, I messed up again and nearly got you killed in the bargain. I sat there reading a book and Spenser came in pointing a shotgun at me. I wasn't ready. I'm so sorry," he said.

"Sounds plausible to me. What were you supposed to do? You couldn't just sit there with a gun trained on the door ready to shoot the first person that entered the jail," Doc said.

"I could have locked the door."

"For Christ sake, it's the jail. How would it look if the law thought they had to lock the door? Wouldn't give me much confidence in them. We saved the county money on a trial," Doc said and forced a grin through gritted teeth.

"I don't know," Zack said dejectedly.

"Zack, you can't always keep bad things from happening. It's just not possible. Evil minds are cunning."

"I must not be evil then because I feel pretty inept."

"I need to lie down. I'm feeling a tad woozy," Doc said as he stretched out on the table.

Mary sat in the corner with her face buried in her hands as she cried.

"I'm going to be fine. Why are you still crying?" Doc asked.

Looking up, Mary said, "I don't know. You scared me to death and you know what you mean to me. What would I do without you?"

"I'm not going to die. Come over here and hold an old man's hand."

Mary walked over and took Doc's hand. As she wiped her tears away with her free hand, the whole

Hamilton family came charging into the office with Blackie bringing up the rear. Kate rushed over to Doc in near hysterics.

"This is exactly why you need to come to Boston and live with us. Somebody is always getting shot here," Kate exclaimed.

"Now is not the time for such talk," John said and eased his wife out of the way.

Doc looked glassy eyed as the stress from being shot began to wear him down. He managed to instruct Henry on how to treat the wound and apply a bandage. By the time Henry finished wrapping the arm, Doc was nodding off.

"I need to rest. I promise I'm going to be fine. I didn't even lose that much blood," Doc mumbled and closed his eyes.

Kate and Mary agreed to watch Doc through the night so Mary left to tell Mrs. Penny that the widow would need to watch Sam until the morning. Zack and John helped the doctor to his bed before Kate shooed them all out of the office.

Zack walked out into the street and picked up Doc's shotgun. "What a day," he said as he headed for the jail.

Chapter 20

The morning after Doc was shot, he mostly slept. He would wake up occasionally and take a small sip of laudanum to ease the pain before dozing back off to sleep. Kate, in a battle of wills, had forced her father-in-law to sit up to eat a bowl of soup that she spoon fed him over his grumblings that he remained capable of feeding himself.

After Zack retrieved his gun belt and revolver at the undertaker's office, he walked over to see Doc. Henry was already there and had removed the bandage from his grandfather's arm. He was in the process of dousing the wound with carbolic acid and iodine when Zack entered the bedroom.

"How does it look?" Zack asked.

"Pretty darn good," Doc said. "Henry is a natural. I'll be up and around in a day or two."

"Do you really think so?" Zack asked skeptically.

"Sure. This arm wound isn't nearly as bad as that time Blackie got shot during the bank robbery. Look how well he healed. Quit your worrying."

The doctor winced in pain as his grandson applied a fresh bandage. Henry, sensing that Zack wanted to talk to Doc alone, finished taping the gauze and excused himself.

"Doc, I feel so responsible for you getting shot. You should have never been put in such a position," Zack said.

"I put myself in that position and I am old enough to know what I was getting into. And you need to quit beating yourself up for all that has happened. I'm not sure one thing would have turned out differently if Gideon had been here. And all in all, I think we're all pretty lucky. As for you, nobody wants to see a deputy walking around acting unsure of himself. I'd put my money on you every time. Now I want you to get out of here and walk around this town as if you own it. And I don't want to hear you doubting yourself again. Do I make myself clear?" Doc said, his voice rising with authority.

Smiling sadly, Zack said, "All right. I'll do my best."

"I'm going to rest now," Doc said, closing his eyes.

Zack moved to the front of the office and found Kate and Henry sitting on the bench. He forced himself to make eye contact with both of them even though he felt sure that they held him responsible for Doc's injury.

As if reading his mind, Kate said, "Zack, no one here blames you. Sometimes things just happen. God knows I'd love to get Doc to move to Boston and away from this violence, but I surely appreciate how all of you stick together and look out for each other."

"Thank you, ma'am. That means a lot to me. I'll see you later," Zack said.

Zack walked down to the Pearl West and entered the saloon. He found all the whores sitting at the tables drinking coffee and in state of agitation. They were the only employees left alive that worked at the establishment and were in a tizzy on what they were going to do.

Not wanting to listen to the women's ire, Zack tried entering Cyrus's office and found it locked. Nobody knew where the key to the room was so Zack kicked in the door. As he looked about the office, he found a bag full of money sitting on the desk. Zack presumed that Cyrus had been reluctant to give Spenser the combination to the safe so the bartender had been forced to lock the receipts in the office. Counting the money, the total came to over two thousand dollars. He divided the money into piles of three hundred dollars and walked back out to where the whores sat with the cash in his hand.

Before he spoke, he thought about Doc telling him to act as if he owned the town. He straightened his posture and pulled back his shoulders. "Ladies, here is three hundred dollars apiece for each of you. You have until the end of the week to take the stagecoach out of town. Any of you that are still here after that will be thrown in jail," he said in a booming voice.

He expected the whores to be up in arms over his directive, but found that the money served as a balm to any concerns they had over where they were to go. As he walked out of the saloon, the women were talking excitedly about what they planned to buy and where they intended to move.

Zack decided that he had better go check on String and Fancy, and to tell them the news about Cyrus. As he rode out of town, he felt as if a burden lifted off his shoulders. He put his mount into a lope and tried not to think about anything but the joy of riding a horse. By the time he reached the Johann homestead, the animal had worked up a lather and he slowed it to a walk the rest of the way to String's cabin.

Figuring that the couple might be on the jumpy side, Zack bellowed, "String, Fancy, it's Zack Barlow."

String and Fancy walked out of the cabin. Fancy appeared none the worse for wear from her ordeal, but

String looked rough. The cowboy appeared dark under the eyes and he squinted in the sunlight.

"How are you all doing?" Zack asked as he climbed off his horse.

"We're getting by. String still has headaches, but the medicine Doc gave him helps some," Fancy answered.

"Glad to hear it. You won't have to testify. Spenser tried to break Cyrus out of jail last night and Doc killed both of them. He nearly got himself killed in the bargain."

Fancy pressed her hands to her lips. They trembled ever so slightly as she did so. String looked down at her and seemingly didn't know what to do. He awkwardly patted her back.

"You're going to be fine," String said as he continued patting her.

Moving her hands away from her mouth, Fancy said, "This is such a relief. You just don't know how much I feared Cyrus. He was such an evil man. I would have quit working for him years ago if I didn't think he'd have tracked me down."

Zack pulled a wad of money out of his pocket. He had already decided that he wouldn't run Fancy out of town since she had been willing to testify and in consideration of all that she had been through. "I found some money at the Pearl West and I gave three hundred dollars to each of the girls there to help get them on their feet. Here is your share," he said and handed Fancy the money.

"Thank you. That's a very generous thing to do."

"Well, I just think it's the right thing to do. What are your plans now?"

Looking up at String, Fancy said, "I don't know yet. I'm going to stay here until I know String is well and then we'll see."

"Best of luck to both of you. I'm going home. It's been a rough couple of days," Zack said.

String extended his hand and shook with Zack. "Thank you for coming out here. I know that Fancy and I will both sleep better tonight," the laconic cowboy said.

Chapter 21

Zack awoke in his own bed for the seventh straight morning since Doc had killed Cyrus and Spenser. He felt the best that he had in a long time. His guilt over all that had gone wrong had lessened to the point that he no longer dwelt on it. Ethan had succinctly pointed out to him that if Doc, String, and Fancy didn't hold him responsible then he should do likewise.

Joann was curled up against him and when he raised his head to look at her, he was surprised to see her looking back at him.

"It's about time you woke up, sleepy head," Joann said.

Looking out the window, Zack realized that he had slept late. "I better get to town since I didn't make an appearance there yesterday."

Throwing her leg over his, Joann said, "Hold on there. I want to talk."

"Can't it wait until tonight?"

"No, it cannot," Joann said matter-of-factly.

Trying not to get annoyed, Zack wondered what could be so all-fired important. He loved his wife dearly, but sometimes her belief that the world revolved around her could get old. "What do you want to talk about?"

"I've decided that I'm ready to have another baby."

Zack dropped his head back onto the pillow and his heartbeat quickened. He hadn't been sure that he would ever hear those words again from his wife. It wasn't as if they were doing anything to prevent a child from coming into the world, but he also knew that there was big difference between Joann accidentally getting pregnant and Joann wanting to get pregnant. "I think that's wonderful."

"Do you really mean it?"

"Of course, I do. You know I want children."

Joann took her finger and ran it down Zack's nose. "Let's make a baby then."

"Right now? Joann, I really need to show my face in town," Zack protested.

Rolling on top of her husband, Joann had her face inches away from his. "You're such a silly man. You would think by now you'd know that Joann Barlow always gets her way," she said and then kissed his mouth before he could speak.

After making love, Joann cooked Zack breakfast while he hastily did the chores. He came in from the barn and shoveled the meal down without bothering to notice the taste of the food.

"I need to get going," Zack said as he stood and put on his hat.

"I'll fix you a good supper. I'm going to need you to keep up your strength," Joann said and gave him a wink.

Back when they first married, Joann's seductive behavior would have embarrassed him to death, but those days were long gone. Thrilled to death to see his old Joann had returned, he raised his eyebrows in exaggeration a couple of times

"I think I'm up to the challenge. I love you," he said and gave his wife a kiss before heading out the door.

Zack loped his horse all the way to town. As he climbed down off the animal, he spotted Doc out of the corner of his eye coming out of his office. The doctor's arm rested in a sling and he used a cane to steady himself while his strength returned, but otherwise, Doc looked remarkably spry for an old codger that had been shot a matter of days ago.

"It's about time you showed up," Doc hollered.

"Is something wrong?" Zack asked as a sense of dread sunk over him.

"No, I just like your coffee better than mine and I haven't had it in a while," Doc said as he shuffled across the street.

"I'll make us a pot as soon as I come back from the Pearl West. I had to let one of the girls stay a few days extra while she awaited word back from St. Louis. She was supposed to leave yesterday. I'm going to lock up the place."

"I'll walk with you."

"Are you sure you're able?"

"Yes, I'm sure. The devil can't catch me as long as I stay moving."

Zack slowed his usual brisk pace to match Doc's slow step and started the half block walk to the saloon. "Did I tell you that Cyrus's lawyer came into the jail before he headed back to Denver blaming me for getting Cyrus killed and causing him to not get paid?" Zack asked.

"If you did, I don't remember. I was a little woozy those first couple of days. That sounds about right for a lawyer though. They're right up there with bankers in my book," Doc said.

"Things sure look better this week than last."

"Yes, they do and you look much relieved. How is Joann?"

Zack looked at the Doc and wondered if the old sage somehow knew why he had been so late in coming to town. "Joann is fine. She told me that she wants to have a baby. There was a time when I sure never thought I'd hear those words from her."

"That's wonderful. I held out hope that she would come around," Doc said as he stepped up onto the boardwalk in front of the saloon.

The two men entered the eerily quiet saloon and looked about the place.

"It's kind of spooky," Zack said.

"Yes, it is. This is an awfully nice saloon to be sitting empty," Doc added.

"I wonder what will happen to it."

"Maybe Mary will buy it after the judge releases it. She has the best head for business in Last Stand. She's liable to own the whole town one of these days."

"Come in here. I want to show you something," Zack said as he walked into Cyrus's office.

"What is it?" Doc asked.

"Look at that safe. I found over two thousand dollars sitting in a bag on the desk. I gave the money to the whores to get them out of town. I bet there's a fortune in that thing," Zack said with wonderment.

"I guess we chose the wrong line of work. If I knew how to open that thing, I'd rob it. We could do a lot for the town with the money," Doc said, grinning.

"That is a tempting idea, but Gideon would probably arrest his own wife and us too for such a thing. I finally found the keys to the doors. Let's lock her up."

After locking the building, Doc and Zack walked back to the jail and the deputy made a pot of coffee as promised. The two men were sitting at the desk sipping from their cups when Ethan, Sarah, and Sylvia walked into the jail.

"There you are," Ethan said to Doc. "How are you feeling?"

"Mean as ever. It takes more than a bullet to slow me down," Doc said.

"Glad to hear it."

Sarah put her hands on Sylvia's shoulders. "I'd like you to meet Sylvia Oakes. The judge just made it all official," she said proudly.

"Congratulations," Doc said.

"That's great news," Zack added.

"We couldn't be happier. She doesn't quite understand what happened, but that's not what matters. She's ours," Sarah gushed.

"Couldn't happen to finer folks," Doc said.

"Have you heard from Gideon and Finnie?" Ethan asked.

"Not a word," Zack replied.

"We will be having a party for Sylvia when they get back," Sarah said.

"We'll be there," Zack promised.

"We need to get home. Glad to see you up and around, Doc," Ethan said as he ushered his family out the door.

Doc drained the last of his coffee. "I better head to the office. My patients think it's high time I get back to work," he said as he used the cane to get to his feet.

"Don't overdo it. We'll still need you around whenever we have another baby," Zack said, smiling at the doctor.

"I've always heard that practice makes perfect," Doc said and winked.

∞

At the end of the working day, Doc locked the door to his office and walked down to Mary's Place to meet his family for dinner. As soon as he took a seat with them, he could sense a nervous energy amongst the group. His family would be heading home in two days and he still hadn't told them of his plans. The usually lively conversations lagged as they ate their meals and there were moments of awkward silence.

Finally, John looked up at his father and said, "Kate and I have talked and we can stay another couple of weeks to allow you to get your strength back to travel home with us."

Doc set his fork down and rubbed his chin. He took a big breath and exhaled before speaking. "John, I'm not going back to Boston. I've come to realize more than ever that Last Stand needs me, and truth be told, maybe I need this town. I love you all dearly, but this is where I need to be."

Kate pulled her shoulders back and lifted her chin. "Doc, we need you too," she pleaded.

"No, you don't need me – you want me to live with you. There's a big difference. Listen, back in Boston I wouldn't know anybody and you all have your own lives to live. Boredom will kill an old codger like me quicker than pneumonia. I'm flattered that you care so much and want me to be a part of your lives, but this is where I belong."

"You won't reconsider?" John asked.

Shaking his head, Doc said, "I just might stick around and keep practicing medicine until Henry graduates from college and then pry him away from Boston.

Maybe I could get the whole lot of you to come with him. You all sure do look good in ranch clothes."

Kate smiled and her eyes welled up with moisture. "We need to make the most of the short time that we still have together," she said and quickly flipped a tear away.

Chapter 22

The sight of Fayetteville, Arkansas coming into view almost seemed like a mirage to Gideon and Finnie. They looked at each other and smiled. Traveling across some of the loneliest and uninhabited land imaginable, there had been times when it felt as if they would never see civilization again. A stop in the small village of Tulsa to resupply had been one of the few times on their journey that the two men had been able to enjoy a decent meal and a bed.

"I'm going to have me a beefsteak the size of a frying pan," Finnie said.

"That sounds about right. And a bath and a shave too," Gideon added.

"Yes, I'm tired of smelling me and you both. Have you had any second thoughts about tracking down the family of the boy?"

"No, I'm going to do it. I figure we'll take care of finding the men we're after and then I'll worry about finding them."

Finnie looked Gideon in the eye and said, "I understand why you feel the need to find that family, but I'll tell you, I have grave reservations about the whole thing."

"Let's get our men and then fret about that. I might get killed before then and save you the worrying," Gideon said, trying to make a joke that fell flat.

Gideon and Finnie rode into the town and left their horses at the livery stable. The blacksmith recommended the Fayetteville Hotel and they took rooms there. Afterwards, they found a barber with a bathhouse. The two men got a shave and a haircut before soaking in tubs until their fingers wrinkled. By that time, the Chinaman that worked in the back of the business had their clothes cleaned and dried by the fire. As they paid their bills, the barber gave them directions to the telegraph office. Gideon sent telegrams to Abby and Zack, and Finnie sent one to Mary.

"The only thing that could make me feel better is some good food," Finnie said as they walked out of the office.

"Well, I say we need to make that happen," Gideon said.

Returning to the hotel, they walked into the dining room. Gideon ordered a T-bone steak and Finnie chose a rib eye. They had spent so much time together on the trail that they talked little except for complimenting the taste of the food. The food hit the spot and they gorged themselves until they couldn't take another bite and had to scoot away from the table.

"Let's go see if we can find the sheriff and let him know why we're here," Gideon said after paying for the meals.

The sheriff's office sat a block down the street from the hotel. As Gideon approached the building, he looked upon it in amazement. The structure had to be three or four times bigger than Last Stand's little jail.

"They must have a lot of criminals around here," Finnie said.

"This is a pretty good sized town," Gideon said before they walked into the building.

Four empty desks made a square in the center of the room and towards the back sat a larger desk surrounded by bookcases with a bearded white haired man sitting at it. "May I help you?" the man asked.

"I'm Sheriff Gideon Johann and this is Deputy Finnie Ford. We're from Last Stand, Colorado and need to talk to the sheriff," Gideon said.

"You're a long ways from home," the man said as he arose and walked over to Gideon and Finnie, shaking their hands. "I'm Sheriff Milton Henry. What can I do for you?"

"We've been in pursuit of Lester and Greg Cole and Howie Elkhart. They killed a man by the name of Rory Kasten back in Last Stand and are also responsible for a train robbery in Kansas years ago," Gideon answered.

The Sheriff Henry seemed taken aback and rubbed his whiskers for a moment. "Are you sure of this?"

"I am. The man they killed took part in the train robbery and ran off with the money. They found Rory and got what remained of the loot. Rory had written out a confession in case such a thing ever happened."

"Those boys left here years ago. The word on them has always been that they struck it big prospecting. Their families have nice things from the money they've sent home," Sheriff Henry said.

"I think they were successful at prospecting other people's money and good at never being identified."

"I know those families well and they are a clannish bunch. It's getting a little late in the day now, but show up here in the morning. We'll ride out there with you and see if those boys are back home."

"Thank you, Sheriff Henry. I appreciate your help."

"Call me Milton. Us lawmen have to stick together. The Red Rooster has the best beer in town if you're so inclined."

"We are inclined. It's been a long ride and we have the sores to prove it. You can call us Gideon and Finnie. No need for formality. See you tomorrow," Gideon said before departing.

Gideon and Finnie found their way down to the saloon and sat at a corner table where both men could have their backs to the wall. Their time as soldiers and lawmen had led them to take precautions without either man even being aware that he did so. They drank a couple of beers apiece before deciding that a real bed would feel better than any more alcohol. The two men retired to their hotel rooms and Gideon could hear Finnie snoring next door before he had even climbed into bed. A few minutes later, he drowned out the sound of his friend with his own snores.

In the morning, the two men met for breakfast in the hotel dining room. Finnie was not only in a festive mood, but also in a hungry one. He managed to scarf down four eggs and a plate full of bacon all while slurping coffee and talking nonstop. Gideon felt much rested and didn't even mind his friend's yapping. He contented himself with his eggs and bacon and would occasionally nod his head or smile when necessary. With the meal finished, they retrieved their horses from the livery stable and walked the animals down to the jail.

Sheriff Milton Henry sat at his desk cleaning his revolver. Two of the other desks were now occupied with deputies.

"Good morning, Gideon and Finnie. You boys look well rested. Are you ready to go see if we can find your men?" Sheriff Henry asked.

"We are well rested and ready to go," Finnie said.

"I'm having Barry and Edgar ride with us."

Looking over at the two deputies, Gideon said, "Do you think we need that many guns?"

"There's a bunch of those Coles and they tend to be on the ornery side. Better extra than not enough."

"I guess I better get some more cartridges before we go if you think this might get real ugly. We're running a little low," Gideon said.

"Go to that cabinet over there and get all that you need. This is law business," Sheriff Henry said and pointed to a wooden bookcase along the wall filled with ammo of all the popular sizes.

Gideon and Finnie each grabbed three boxes of .44-40 cartridges before following the Fayetteville lawmen out of the jail. The men mounted up and began riding north out of town through farmland. As they rode, Gideon and Finnie told the men of their days together fighting in the war and reuniting to become the sheriff and deputy of Last Stand. Gideon skipped telling of his time drifting across the west or killing the boy. Sheriff Henry talked of his days of fighting for the Confederacy. Nobody seemed surprised or to care that they had fought on opposite sides during the war.

After riding for a little over an hour, Sheriff Henry turned up a driveway that led to a nice two-story white clapboard house. A couple of men could be seen working in a nearby field and two others were repairing a plow by the barn. The eldest man stood and wiped his hands with a rag at seeing the approaching men.

"Milton, what brings you out here?" the man asked as he ran his hand through his long gray beard and eyed the lawmen.

"Fletcher, I heard that Lester, Greg, and Howie are back here and I need to talk to them," Milton said.

"And who are you?" Fletcher asked Gideon.

"Sheriff Johann from Colorado," Gideon said.

"So what is this all about?" Fletcher inquired.

Sheriff Henry moved his horse up a step in front of the other lawmen. "I need to question them about a murder in Colorado and a train robbery in Kansas," Milton said.

"Those aren't your jurisdictions. You should worry about your own county," Fletcher said as he tossed the rag onto the ground.

"Upholding the law is my job."

"What you are really saying is that you've come to arrest my boys and Howie."

"No, I want to talk to them first and hear their side of the story. Where are they?"

"I'm not in the habit of giving up my kin to the law, especially my sons," Fletcher said before spitting on the ground.

"Fletcher, we've known each other a long time and you know that I'm fair. If I have to track down your boys, somebody is liable to get hurt. Do you want that?" Milton asked.

"I'm done talking," Fletcher said and turned back to the plow.

"Let's go," Sheriff Henry said and turned his horse.

As the lawmen rode way, Gideon asked, "Are we going to get shot in the back?"

"Nah, Fletcher might still try to kill us, but he's not the type to bushwhack. Just keep riding," the sheriff said.

A quarter of a mile down the road, a row of hedge apples served as a natural fence and property line. The men rode past the trees into a swale deep enough to hide them from the Cole farmhouse.

Sheriff Henry held his hand up for the men to stop. "Barry, hold all the horses. The rest of us can walk to the hedgerow and do a little spying."

Gideon retrieved his spyglass from his saddlebag before climbing off Buck. The four men jogged farther down the swale before walking out of it behind the trees. Through his spyglass, Gideon could see Fletcher standing with the two men that had been working in the field and with the other man that had been helping repair the plow.

"The one that was helping Fletcher just climbed on a horse," Gideon said.

The lawmen watched as the man rode northwest.

"That's Peyton. His house and the Elkhart home are to the northwest. We can ride down this hedgerow and hit the road that leads to both places. I expect wherever Peyton goes, we'll find our men," Sheriff Henry said.

They put the horses into a lope as Sheriff Henry led the way down the row of trees until they came upon the road. Turning north, the lawmen continued riding. They came upon the spot where Peyton had taken to road. His speeding horse had kicked up easy to follow tracks in the dusty road.

"He's headed to his place," Sheriff Henry called out after following the tracks past a side road.

As Peyton Cole's house came into view, Sheriff Henry slowed his horse to a walk. "I'm going to ride up to the house and try to talk to them. Two of you can head for that timber on the left and the other two can arc around to the back. There's a creek back there with banks deep enough to take cover in. I sure hope we can do this without bloodshed."

Barry flinched as if he had a cold chill, and a tick of a clock later, the sound of the gunshot reached the lawmen.

"Head for the woods," Sheriff Henry yelled as he spurred his horse.

Gideon was the nearest rider to Barry and tried to reach down to grab the bridle of the deputy's horse just as the injured man slumped over the horse's neck. The startled animal shied away and Gideon turned Buck to make another attempt to lead the deputy to safety. Barry's horse bolted a few yards away and stood there as Barry's blood ran down its shoulder. Gideon's horse let out an ear-piercing squeal as another rifle shot rang out. Buck's knees slowly buckled and forced Gideon to dismount as the animal collapsed. As Buck rolled onto his side, Gideon squatted to retrieve his ammo and to pull his rifle from the scabbard. As Gideon stood, he looked Buck in the eye and froze. The horse gazed at him in fear and pain. Gideon became oblivious to his surroundings and to the danger that he faced. He thought about all that he and Buck had been through together back when he didn't have a friend in the world. Buck had been the most loyal and trustworthy animal he had ever owned and he had no intention to leave him to die alone.

Finnie looked over his shoulder as he and the other lawmen raced for the woods and saw Gideon standing over his horse. The Irishman spun his mount around and charged back towards Gideon as another shot sounded.

"Gideon, hold out your arm and I'll get you," Finnie yelled.

If Gideon heard him or the gunshot, he showed no sign of it. He remained standing like a statue. As Finnie neared his friend, he slowed his horse and jumped from the saddle while gripping one of the reins. He tackled Gideon to the ground with a thud.

"What in the hell are you doing?" Gideon yelled.

"Trying to keep you from getting killed. Let's get out of here," Finnie yelled back as he climbed off Gideon.

"I'm not leaving Buck," Gideon said, his voice flat and monotone.

"Gideon, put him out of his misery. Don't let him suffer."

"I can't do that."

Reaching for his revolver, Finnie said, "Let me do it for you."

Gideon grabbed Finnie's hand before the gun had cleared the leather. "No, that horse never quit on me once and I'll be damned if I'll quit on him. Maybe he'll survive, but if he doesn't, I'll not let him die alone. Get on your horse and get to the trees."

"You know I'm not leaving you. We'll stay here hunkered down," Finnie said as he pulled his horse close and quickly retrieved his rifle.

Sheriff Henry and Deputy Edgar had reached the timber and were firing upon the house. The return fire had forced the men inside the home to turn their attention away from Gideon and Finnie and toward the woods. The two sides continued to exchange shots, but at a distance of nearly a hundred yards, nobody had hit their target.

Gideon rubbed Buck's neck and seemed to be lost in thought. A horse nickered, and Finnie glanced up to see that Barry's mount had returned to within a couple of steps of him and Gideon. Finnie handed Gideon the rein to his horse before shimming towards Barry's animal and grabbing the rein lying on the ground. He quickly popped to his feet and used the horse as a shield as he checked Barry for a pulse.

"Barry is dead," Finnie said.

A moment passed before the news seemed to register with Gideon. He looked up blankly towards Finnie. "I thought it looked bad," he said.

Finnie reached under the horse and pulled Barry's boot from the stirrup. He did the same on his nearside and pushed the deputy from the saddle. "Hate to do that, but we've got two horses now."

"Buck is gone. Finnie, my horse is dead," Gideon said as he continued to stroke the animal's neck.

Finnie flopped back down on the ground next to Gideon. He didn't say anything for a moment. Finally, he said, "Gideon, I'm truly sorry about Buck, but now is not the time to grieve. You need to focus on the job at hand or you're liable to get either me or you killed. We both have too many people depending on us to die today. Let's get this over with."

Finnie's words brought Gideon out of his daze and he nodded his head in agreement. Without another word being said, they jumped onto the horses and made a mad sprint for the trees. Sheriff Henry and Edgar began a barrage of shots at the house, preventing the outlaws from taking more than a couple of shots at the racing lawmen. After reaching the cover of the trees, Gideon and Finnie tied their horses with the other two mounts as Sheriff Henry and Edgar met them at the rear of the woods.

"Barry is dead," Finnie said.

"I figured as much. Barry had a wife and two kids, and I considered him a friend. Those boys have made this real personal now," Sheriff Henry said.

"That's how I feel about them killing my horse," Gideon said.

Sheriff Henry looked at Gideon in surprise. Horses had never been more than a means of transportation to him and he found the statement odd. Deciding to ignore Gideon's statement, he said, "That was a brave thing you did trying to rescue Barry. I admire that in a man."

Nodding his head, Gideon didn't respond.

"So do you have a plan?" Finnie asked.

"I thought that maybe you and Gideon could work your way around to the other side. We'd have them covered from two directions if they got to the barn and try to make a run for it. We're going to have to keep an eye out for Fletcher and the rest of the family showing up here. I don't like our odds if they do. We've got a lot of daylight left," Sheriff Henry said.

Gideon started walking towards the front of the woods in the direction of the house.

"What's he doing?" Sheriff Henry asked Finnie.

"I don't have a clue," Finnie replied.

Peyton Cole's horse stood tied by the side of the house. Gideon braced himself against a tree and aimed his Winchester at the animal. He lightly exhaled and squeezed the trigger. The horse dropped to the ground without so much as a kick.

"He's really upset, isn't he?" Sheriff Henry asked.

"You have no idea. He was attached to that horse."

Gideon returned without saying anything and began adjusting the stirrups on Barry's horse to fit his height. "Finnie, let's work our way around to the back of the house," he said as he mounted up.

As Finnie climbed upon his horse, Sheriff Henry said, "If we haven't got them by nightfall, let's meet up at the back of the barn. I'll whistle as we approach and you do the same."

Without acknowledging the sheriff's remarks, Gideon asked, "Is there any chance of women or children being inside of that house?"

"Peyton is unmarried, so I wouldn't think so," Sheriff Henry replied.

Gideon lightly heeled the horse into moving and rode away without saying another word.

After riding out of hearing range of Sheriff Henry and his deputy, Finnie said, "You've got something else up your sleeve, don't you?"

Smiling sadly, Gideon said, "My little Irishman, you know me well. Finnie, I'm in no mood to dillydally. I want to get done what we came for and go home," Gideon said without giving any details.

The two men continue riding in a wide arc that put them well out of rifle range of the outlaws. Occasionally a round of shots between the outlaws and Sheriff Henry and his deputy would break the silence. Finnie decided it best to leave Gideon to his own thoughts and didn't pester him with questions or the nonsense he loved to use to rile his friend. They rode until Gideon stopped directly behind the barn nearly a quarter of a mile away. From their position, the view of the house was completely obliterated by barn.

"I figure we'll just ride up to the barn, swoop around it, jump off our horses, and surprise the hell out of them," Gideon said.

Finnie let out a sigh. "What if somebody is watching out a side window?" he asked.

"Well, I'd expect that with both of us shooting at him that we'd shoot him before he shot us."

"Might kind of ruin the element of surprise," Finnie remarked.

"Listen, if you think it's too dangerous, I'll go it alone. I don't want you doing something that you think is folly,."

Turning his horse, Finnie began riding towards the barn and Gideon did the same. They rode at an easy pace until they reached the barn and stopped.

"I hope that sheriff is smart enough to take some shots to distract them for us. I'm not too sure about him. We'll ride to the side and then run onto the porch. I'll take the first window and you can check the second. After that I figure I'll bust in the door and we'll see what happens," Gideon said.

"Gideon, don't get yourself killed just because you're feeling careless right now," Finnie pleaded.

"Don't you worry about that. Getting killed is just the opposite of what I have on my mind," Gideon said as he drew his revolver and spurred his horse.

They reached the side of the house with no sign that the outlaws were any the wiser. Sheriff Henry and Edgar began firing their rifles as Gideon and Finnie jumped from their mounts and dashed around to the front porch. A rifle protruded from the first window, firing towards the timberline. Gideon grabbed the hot barrel, forcing it to the side as he shoved his Colt through the opening and fired. The barrel of the revolver nearly touched the man's chest as it discharged and the force of the impact sent the outlaw sliding across the floor. Gideon quickly released the rifle and rubbed his stinging hand against his trousers as Finnie found the second window unoccupied. They crawled under the window, hugging the wall and reached the door. The two windows on the opposite of the entrance no longer showed rifles pointed from them.

Taking a breath and exhaling, Gideon said, "Let's get this over with."

Gideon took two steps back before crashing his shoulder into the door. As the doorjamb gave way, he let his momentum carry him to the floor. While sliding across the wood surface, he tried to view the whole room before he came to a stop. He spotted a man standing in the corner by the window with his rifle held to his chest. As the man tried to get out of his own way to take aim upon the sheriff, Gideon fired two shots into the man. The outlaw slid down the walls having never gotten his gun in position to fire. Finnie stood in the doorway with his revolver cocked and ready to take aim at the first sign of movement. He didn't have long to wait as another man came charging in from a room off to the right with his revolver drawn. Finnie fired instantly. He had intended for a chest shot, but led his moving target a little too much and the bullet hit the outlaw's upper right arm near the shoulder. The revolver dropped from the man's hand as he screamed in pain and his knees buckled.

As Gideon got back on his feet, he snatched up the outlaw's gun while watching the doorways, but the house had gone deathly still. "Peyton, crawl into the front room on your hands and knees or you're going to get shot just like all the rest," he bellowed.

A moment later, Peyton could be heard moving in the back of the house. Gideon and Finnie stood side by side with their revolvers pointed towards the rear entrance of the room as Peyton appeared on all fours moving towards them.

"Don't shoot me. I didn't do any of the shooting. I just did as my Pa told me to let them know the law was after them," Peyton called out. The fear on his face betrayed his doubt that the lawmen intended to let him live.

"Lie down on your belly with your arms out to your sides. Do you have a weapon?" Gideon asked.

Peyton did as he was told. "Just a pocketknife," he answered.

Gideon walked into the room on the left side of the house and checked on the first man that had been shot. "This one is dead," he called out.

"So is the one in the corner," Finnie said.

"Which one are you?" Gideon asked the outlaw that still stood on his knees and held his wounded arm.

"I'm Lester," he said through teeth gritted in pain.

"Finnie, see if you can put a tourniquet on his arm and I'll wave the sheriff in," Gideon said as he headed out the door.

By the time that Sheriff Henry and Deputy Edgar had arrived at the home, Finnie had a kerchief knotted around the wounded man's arm and had slowed the bleeding considerably. Lester sat on the floor with his back to the wall mere feet from his dead brother. He seemed too preoccupied with his own injury to be overly concerned with the fate of his brother or cousin.

"You boys don't piss around," Sheriff Henry said as he stepped into the house and looked at the carnage.

"Killing a deputy and my horse will cause such things," Gideon said matter-of-factly before pointing at a pair of saddlebags. "There is what's left of the money from the Kansas train robbery."

"Where's Howie?" the sheriff asked.

"He's dead in that room there," Gideon said he as pointed with his hand.

Sheriff Henry glanced over at Peyton sitting on the floor. "Your pa should have listened to me. Greg and Howie would still be alive if he had."

"We need to get this one to a doctor. I can't get the bleeding completely stopped," Finnie said after applying a second tourniquet.

Sheriff Henry turned to Edgar. "Go saddle up five horses if they have them. We'll need three for bodies and two for Lester and Peyton," he said.

"I didn't raise a gun at nobody. I just came home and told them the law was looking for them," Peyton protested.

"I'm throwing you in jail anyway and I'll decide what I'm going to do with you later," the sheriff said.

"I'll ride a horse bareback to my saddle so that I can get it back to town," Gideon said to Edgar before the deputy walked out of the house.

"Gideon, I'm not going to be able to let you take Lester back to Colorado now. He'll have to stand trial for the murder of Barry. If he's convicted, I expect he'll swing. They don't call Isaac Parker the hanging judge for nothing. I'll personally deliver him to you if he's not," Sheriff Henry said.

"As long as justice is served, I don't give a damn," Gideon said.

"I didn't shoot your deputy. Greg shot him," Lester complained.

"The court will decide that. You all were shooting at us, I believe. Just shut up before I make it hard for you to talk," Sheriff Henry said.

Gideon pulled his Colt from his holster and reloaded the gun. "I'm going to take a walk to the barn and see if I can find a shovel."

"Make it two," Finnie said.

Sheriff Henry looked at the two men with confusion. "I don't understand," he said.

"I have to bury Buck," Gideon said before walking out the door.

Chapter 23

Gideon slept in to nearly eight o'clock on the morning after capturing Lester Cole. He and Finnie had exhausted themselves the night before digging a hole big enough in which to bury Buck. By the time they had returned to the hotel, the dining room had closed and they felt too tired to look for food elsewhere. Both men had collapsed into bed not caring about a growling belly.

After Gideon dressed, he strolled downstairs and into the dining room, finding Finnie reading a newspaper and sipping coffee. A waitress had already cleared away the Irishman's plate.

"Top of the morning to you, my sleeping beauty. I was too hungry to wait for you," Finnie said.

"I don't blame you," Gideon said as he sat down at the table.

Finnie beamed as if the day were one of his best. Gideon smiled as he allowed himself to admit that he admired the Irishman's enthusiasm for life. He also knew that he had a near perfect partner. Sure, Finnie could get on his last nerve, but his deputy always proved as sure and steady as they came. The night before, the Irishman had worked every bit as hard as he had at digging and never complained once. Singing Irish ballads the whole evening had been his worst offense, and even then, Gideon had to allow that Finnie had a fine voice.

"I can tell I haven't used a shovel in a good while. I'm sore this morning," Finnie said.

Gideon ordered his breakfast and then said, "Finnie, thank you for helping me bury Buck. You didn't have to do that and I appreciate it."

"You are welcome. You didn't have to bring a drunk back from Animas City to sober up and make him your deputy either, but you did."

Letting out a chuckle, Gideon said, "All right, enough of this or people are going to start talking about us."

Grinning, Finnie said, "Sounds good to me."

Gideon took his spoon and stirred his coffee for a moment before looking up at Finnie. "I don't think I ever told you that I won Buck in a poker game. This cowboy tried to get me to accept his wager and said that he had a three-year-old gelding with the smoothest gait he had ever ridden. Said he was a fine cattle horse, too. I figured he was just talking, but I took him up on the bet. I planned to sell the horse. Well, I took one ride on Buck and knew I would be keeping him. He proved to be as fine of a cattle horse as the cowboy said he was. I guess I've had Buck nine years. That horse and I have been through so much together. He remained the only constant in my life for a long time. I don't suppose I'll ever have another like him," he mused.

"Gideon, I'm truly sorry you lost Buck. I know he meant the world to you. The special ones don't come along very often. I haven't had one since that gelding I had in the war."

"I know. It's just so strange to think that he's gone."

"I've been thinking that I've never been crazy about that horse that Blackie sold me. He's a little too skittish for my taste. I could see if the livery stable would buy him. We could sell them the packhorse too and pay Blackie for him. I don't think Blackie would mind. We could then take the train back to Colorado. What do you think?" Finnie asked.

The waitress brought Gideon a plate of eggs, bacon, and ham. He waited until she left before speaking. "I think that's a fine idea. We've had our butts in a saddle enough for a while. I won't have to listen to you worrying about Indians all the way across the Oklahoma Territory that way either."

Grinning, Finnie said, "My hair is too pretty to be hanging from some brave's spear."

Gideon took a bite of ham and chewed the meat slowly. "I thought I'd get a bath and a shave before we go see Sheriff Henry. I'm going to see if he knows anything about the boy's family. If he does, I thought I'd use your horse to ride out there today."

"Hold on a minute. You can't go by yourself. That's a good way to get yourself killed. Abby and Mary would never forgive me if something happened to you and I wasn't there to help," Finnie protested.

"Finnie, I have to do this by myself. It's the right thing to do. I'm not going to stand there and let somebody gun me down – I promise. I've made up my mind about this and won't be swayed."

Finnie sighed loud enough that a couple at the next table looked over at him. "You never make life easy on the rest of us," he said and dropped the subject.

As they left the dining room, the hotel clerk waved them over and handed them telegrams.

"Mary says that all is fine," Finnie said.

"That's more or less the same thing that Abby and Zack sent me. Everybody seems kind of vague. What do you think that means?" Gideon asked.

Thinking for a moment, Finnie said, "If I had to guess, I would say that all hell broke out but things are fine now."

"I wonder if you are right. I'm sure Zack was up to the challenge if it's so. I guess we'll find out when we get home."

After going to their rooms for clean clothes, Gideon and Finnie returned to the barbershop for a bath and a shave. When they finished, they walked down to the jail and entered the building. Sheriff Henry arose from his desk and greeted them as soon they came through the door.

"I thought maybe you two headed back home without a goodbye," the sheriff said.

"No, we're just moving a little slow today," Gideon replied.

"I turned Peyton loose. There wasn't any point in ruining his life for following his pa's orders. Fletcher came in here first thing. I told him he had no one to blame but his self for getting Greg and Howie killed. He didn't take that any too well, but turning Peyton over to him seemed to appease him a bit. I also don't believe he had any idea that his sons were thieves and murderers," Sheriff Henry said.

Gideon looked down at his feet and rubbed the back of his neck with his hand. Realizing that he was headed down a path from which he could never come back, he carried on an internal conversation in his head before speaking. "Sheriff, you've lived in these parts all your life, haven't you?"

"Sure, except for my years in the Confederacy."

"When you got back, did you ever hear of a boy found shot in November of '64. There were some skirmishes around here against Major-General Sterling Price."

Sheriff Henry pulled his head back and looked Gideon in the eyes. "The Irby boy was found shot dead. Gideon, why are you asking about this after all this time?"

"Milton, I know what happened to the boy. Is there family still around these parts? I want to let them know what happened."

"Sure, Thomas and Addie Irby and their sons have a farm northwest of town. I can take you out there."

"I think I need to go there by myself. If you could give me directions, I'd be much obliged."

"If that's what you prefer," the sheriff said and proceeded to give Gideon directions. Sheriff Henry was dying to ask more questions, but out of his respect for Gideon, he kept his mouth shut.

Gideon thanked the sheriff before he and Finnie began walking to the livery stable.

"I'm begging you to let me go with you," Finnie said.

"Finnie, I have to do this alone. I promise you that I'm not going to stand there and let them shoot me. I have too much to live for now," Gideon said.

Letting out a sigh, the Irishman didn't say anything else. He retrieved his horse from the livery and held out the reins to Gideon. Before taking them, Gideon unfastened his watch fob and handed it and the pocket watch to Finnie.

"If something were to happen, please make sure that Chance gets this. It was my pa's watch and I want to pass it down to my son."

Finnie took a breath and blew it out loudly His eyes moistened and his hand trembled ever so slightly as he took the watch. "Gideon, you're scaring me."

"Everything is going to be just fine," Gideon said and then he shook Finnie's hand. "I'll see you later."

While navigating Sheriff Henry's directions, Gideon traveled toward the Irby farm. He scanned the terrain as he rode, trying to find a landmark that he remembered. Back during the war, life had been lived at such a hectic pace with continuous movement. Gideon realized that he had no recollection of the land. After almost an hour, he came upon the road to the Irby farm. As he rode up the driveway, he admired the big house with lots of towering oaks in the yard. He came upon the family cemetery beside the road. The realization that one of the headstones was of the boy that he had killed made his heart start racing and he could feel sweat running down his sides. He tried to calm himself, but his hands were shaking and he felt lightheaded. After all these years, he and the boy were reunited.

Four men were unhitching a mule and pushing a sickle mower into a shed. The time was nearing noon and they were apparently getting ready to go have lunch. Gideon rode up to the men and they looked up in surprise when his horse nickered at the mule.

"Can I help you?" the oldest of the men asked.

The man looked to be about sixty with gray hair and weather beaten skin from a life in the sun. He wore bib overalls and a straw hat. Gideon searched his face trying to see a resemblance to the image of the boy that had been seared into his brain. The eyes were the same as those he had seen thousands of times when he had tried to go to sleep back in the lost years.

"Are you Thomas Irby?" Gideon asked.

"I am," Thomas said.

Climbing down from the horse, Gideon said, "I need to talk to you. My name is Gideon Johann. I'm the sheriff of Last Stand, Colorado."

"I've never even been to Colorado," Thomas interrupted as if he expected the sheriff to accuse him of a crime out west. The four Irby men had formed a line in front of Gideon as he had their undivided attention.

"This isn't about anything that happened in Colorado. I fought for the Union in this area during the war. Some of us were separated from our unit. I was the leader of the group and I heard something crashing through the brush. The Rebs were bad about guerilla attacks like that and that's what I thought was happening," Gideon said and paused. He took a big breath and exhaled slowly. "I fired my gun into the brush. Mr. Irby, I'm the man that killed your son."

Thomas Irby's body began to quiver all over. His face contorted into a mask of pain and surprise. Gideon feared the man might be having a stroke. The three sons seemed too dumbfounded to move or to offer assistance to their father. Mr. Irby squatted to the ground.

"Mr. Irby, are you all right?" Gideon asked as he bent over and placed his hand on the father's shoulder.

One of the sons suckered punched Gideon in the temple. The blow sent Gideon to the ground and put him in a fog. He reached for his revolver, but a foot pinned his arm to the ground. Somebody gave him a couple of vicious kicks in the ribs and another grabbed his Colt. Two of the brothers seized Gideon by the arms and yanked him to his feet.

Thomas Irby had managed to get back to standing on his feet with the help of his third son. His body still shook and he leaned against the wheel of the sickle mower for support. "Hang him," he said.

Gideon attempted to break free, but the two men body slammed him to the ground and bound his hands behind his back. The other son removed Finnie's lariat from the horse and began making a noose.

"Don't bother with a noose. Just make a slipknot. I want him to strangle to death," Thomas ordered.

The son did as he was told and tossed the rope over a limb of one of the towering oaks in the yard. The other two lifted Gideon onto the saddle of Finnie's horse and led the animal under the rope.

Gideon looked down at the men and realized that the battle was lost. He didn't have any fight left in him anyway. Truth be told, he wondered if he didn't deserve to be hanged. He very well might have done the same thing if the situation was reversed. As they put the rope around his neck, he closed his eyes and pictured Abby, Joann, Winnie, and Chance.

"Lunch is ready," a woman called out from the veranda of the home. "What is going on?"

"Addie, get back in the house," Thomas ordered.

"I want to know what is going on here. Since when did we become the law?" Addie protested, alarm sounding in her voice.

"This man showed up and says that he's the one that killed Peter. Now go back inside while we give him what he deserves," Thomas said.

Gideon opened his eyes and watched Mrs. Irby come marching towards her family like a woman on a mission. Her arms churned by her sides and her eyes were locked onto her husband.

"You are not hanging anybody until I hear with my own ears what this man has to say. I haven't waited all these years to learn what happened to Peter and be denied now that the truth is here. Now get him down off that horse," Addie ordered as she stopped in front of Finnie's mount.

The sons looked towards their father for guidance and Thomas nodded his head. One of the sons removed the rope from Gideon's neck and the other two yanked him from the horse. The two brothers stood on either side of Gideon and each held an arm firmly in their grasp.

"Let go of him. I don't think he can do much harm with his hands tied behind his back," Addie instructed.

The two sons did as they were told and stepped back a step.

"What's your name?" Addie asked.

Gideon told her his name.

"I want to hear every single thing that you can remember from that day," Addie said.

Repeating what he had already told the woman's husband, Gideon paused to let her take in all he had said. Her eyes were welling with tears, but she seemed composed.

"Did he suffer?" Addie asked.

"He lived a few minutes. And ma'am, I'm not going to lie to you. His eyes were filled with fear. I held his hand and asked him his name, but he couldn't speak. I told him how sorry I was and I held his hand until he died.

Ma'am, we were in a war and we had to leave," Gideon said.

Addie's shoulder began to tremble and a sob that she tried to stymie with her fist escaped her. Thomas found the strength to walk over and put his arm around his wife.

"The thought of little Peter suffering is almost more than I can bear," Addie said when she was ready to speak again.

"Mrs. Irby, the loss of his life proved to be almost more than I could stand. It nearly ruined my own life," Gideon said.

"Why are you here after all this time?" Addie asked.

"Ma'am, I never returned home after the war. I spent the next fourteen years drifting. Actually running from what I had done. Most nights when I closed my eyes, I'd see your son's eyes staring at me. I led a miserable life. A few years ago, I chased some rustlers to near my hometown and got shot. I was about dead when the son of my childhood best friend found me. I hadn't seen any of these people from Last Stand since I left for the war. Those people nursed me back to health and helped me put the past behind me. I married my old sweetheart and had a son," Gideon said and paused to gather himself after his voice cracked with emotion. "I came to believe that it was the hand of God that had intervened on my behalf. I'm now the sheriff of Last Stand. Even back in the lost years I thought about coming here, but I never could find the nerve. I've always had coming back here on my mind. The actual doing it proved to be the hard part. I had to chase some outlaws to this area and I decided that God must be telling me that the time had come to find you."

Addie needed to sit down and she instructed one of her sons to retrieve a chair. Once she had taken a seat, she asked, "Did you come here seeking forgiveness?"

Gideon took a big breath and blew up his cheeks as he exhaled. "Sure, that's what I hoped. I'm not sure that's what I expected. Taking a life is a mighty big thing to come seeking forgiveness for – especially a child's. I certainly never intended to take his life."

"Are you a good man, Mr. Johann?" Addie inquired.

Sighing, Gideon managed a small smile. "I believe I am. I know that I try to do the right thing. My best friend is a preacher, and Ethan is always telling me that God sent me home to be his burden. If you hang me, I'm not afraid to die. I should have been dead years ago. I only regret what it will do to my family."

Mrs. Irby began patting the bun her hair was done up in. She looked as if she were using the time to think. "Little Tom, untie Mr. Johann's hands," she said.

"Ma," Little Tom objected.

"Addie, what are you thinking? This man nearly destroyed us. Have you forgotten all the pain and grieving?" Thomas asked his wife.

"It sounds to me as if Mr. Johann did more grieving over Peter than we did. We never lost fourteen years of our lives, and after the hurting stopped, we got on with living. We have always been a good Christian family and I must forgive a man that came here seeking forgiveness. We'd be making a mockery of going to church all these years if we didn't. That silly war is the real blame. Now the four of you had better find it in your heart to forgive him, too. If you can't, then I've failed as a mother and as a wife," Addie said.

The four men shuffled their feet uneasily and looked at each other for signs of what the others were thinking.

"Little Tom, untie his hands. Your ma is right. If I truly believe what the church has been teaching me, well, then I have to forgive him," Thomas said.

The three sons looked as if their father's forgiveness was enough for them to follow his lead. They visibly relaxed as Little Tom untied Gideon's hands and handed him his Colt.

"Mr. Johann, would you please have lunch with us?" Addie asked.

"Please call me Gideon."

"Gideon, would you please break bread with my family?" Addie repeated.

"If your family is willing, then I'd be honored," Gideon replied.

While the meal would have never been mistaken for a homecoming, it still went better than Gideon would have guessed. Thomas talked mostly of their farm. Each son volunteered information about his wife and children. Gideon did the same, talking of his shock of learning that he had a grown daughter and of the death of his granddaughter Tess. Addie finally broached the subject that everyone tried to dance around and talked about Peter, the baby of the family. What tension still existed in the room vanished when the men were drawn into telling tales about Peter. The family began laughing at the memories of the child's exploits. By the time the meal was finished, Gideon looked around the room and decided that the remarkable family before him had truly forgiven him.

Gideon shook each of the men's hand as he prepared to leave. "Would it be possible for me to visit Peter's grave before I left?" he asked.

Addie took Gideon by the hand. "I'll walk you out there."

As they walked to the family cemetery, Gideon said, "I wish I would have been brave enough to come here years ago. All of us would probably have been better off."

"That may well be, but I believe God has his own timetable and knows what is best for all of us. Maybe I would have let them hang you in the past. I've spent so many hours wondering about Peter's death. I'll be able to go to sleep tonight knowing that he wasn't alone in his final moments. I've worried about that for so long. You did the best that you could. We're all human."

"Thank you. Your forgiveness has freed me from my last burden."

Addie led Gideon to Peter's headstone. She gave Gideon a hug. "God's speed, Gideon," she said before walking back to the house.

Gideon sat down on the ground next to the headstone and placed his hand atop the marker. He seemed at a loss for words, but could feel the emotional dam that had been building start to give way. Sobs began to rack his body. He shed tears for Peter, for himself and his lost years, for all the suffering that people had endured for his one careless moment, for Buck, and for the joy of finally having the final burden of the death of Peter Irby lifted from his soul.

Chapter 24

Gideon shook his head with dismay at Finnie. "You are absolutely relentless. I promise I will tell you what happened when I'm ready to talk about my visit with the Irby family. I'm not trying to be difficult, but I just don't want to do it yet. Please give me a little privacy," he pleaded with Finnie.

Finnie let out a sigh, realizing that he had mistaken Gideon's need for silence for plain old hardheadedness. "All right. I'm sorry. Curiosity got the better of me."

"Let's go tell Sheriff Henry goodbye before we catch the train," Gideon suggested.

The two men walked to the jail burdened with their saddles and belongings. The sheriff sat at his desk reading the *Arkansas Democrat* newspaper. He peered over the top of the paper as Gideon and Finnie approached him.

"Are you two boys heading back west?" Sheriff Henry asked.

"We are. I just wanted to tell you goodbye and to thank you for all your help," Gideon said.

"Like I said, us lawmen have got to stick together and it's been good to meet the both of you. I'll be sure to send you a telegram after Lester's trial. Have a safe trip," the sheriff said.

"You take care," Finnie said.

The train station sat several blocks from the jail. After lugging their possessions all the way there, they checked them and boarded the St. Louis & San

Francisco Railway train. Fifteen minutes later, the train left the station.

"It's been a long time since I rode a train. I forgot what it feels like," Finnie said as he tried to get used to the feel of the moving car.

"Me too, but it sure should beat riding a horse all the way back to Colorado," Gideon conceded.

"A train is kind of like the whore that told the man that as long as he had the wood then she had the steam to go, go, go all night."

Gideon started giggling and slapped his thigh with his hand. "You kill me," he said.

"Was it that funny?"

"No, it wasn't funny at all, but you sure are. Sometimes I forget how dull life would be without you entertaining all of us."

Finnie wasn't sure whether to take Gideon's words as a compliment or an insult. He smiled nonetheless and said, "We Irish can do it all."

Turning somber, Gideon looked out the window and watched the landscape pass by his view. So many miles stretched ahead and he was so ready to be home. He felt conflicted. Meeting the Irby family had freed him from his last vestige of guilt and he realized that their forgiveness should be enough to give him peace of mind, but losing Buck still seemed to suck the life out of him. He knew that a lot of men would probably laugh him down for being sentimental over a horse, but most men hadn't spent years keeping their own company with one horse being their only constant companion. Overwhelmed with the mixed feelings, Gideon closed his eyes and drifted off to sleep.

Gideon awoke when the car crossed an uneven spot in the track and shook. He opened his eyes to see Finnie reading a magazine he'd purchased.

"They almost hanged me," Gideon said.

"What? Who?" Finnie asked as he tried to follow the conversation.

"The Irby family – at least the father and brothers of the boy. If the mother hadn't stepped outside, I'd be dead now."

"Oh, Gideon, I'm sorry. Are you all right?"

"I am. Mrs. Irby heard my story and forgave me. That woman is a good Christian lady. She got her family to see to her way of thinking, too. Things ended well, but there was a moment where all I could picture was Abby taking care of Winnie and Chance all by herself."

"At least you made your peace with the family and we'll be home soon. You won't have to trouble your mind with such things ever again."

"That is exactly what I intend to do. I just wanted to tell you about what happened. I'm not going to tell anybody else so keep it under your hat," Gideon said.

"You have my word," Finnie said.

"Seeing Peter's grave seemed so strange. It was as if I had made this huge circle back to where things went all so wrong. So many people paid so dearly for my actions and that damn old war."

"The journey is complete now. It's time to move on with your life," Finnie said as he reached over and tapped Gideon's leg for emphasis.

"You are right on both counts," Gideon said before looking out the window and watching the landscape again.

The long train ride into Missouri, across Kansas to Denver, and then south to Alamosa seemed like an endless series of train stations and water stops. For the normally active Gideon and Finnie, the days on end of riding became torture. Both of them would annoy other passengers with their constant pacing up and down the cars. They occasionally played cards with other passengers, but cabin fever had gripped them to the point that neither man could play for very long. By the time they climbed off the train in Alamosa, both swore that they would never ride another train for as long as they lived.

After dining with Sheriff White and spending the night in Alamosa, they boarded the stage for home early the next morning. As Last Stand came into view, Finnie let out a whoop and Gideon grinned like a child in a candy store. They climbed out of the stage, grabbed their belongings, and started walking up the street. As they reached the Last Chance, they stopped.

Gideon dropped his saddle and held out his hand. "I'm always giving you a hard time and probably don't appreciate you enough, but thank you for all you did on this trip. I don't know what I would have done without you," he said.

After shaking hands, Finnie said, "I'm kind of like the ugly whore that's good at her trade. Every time her john is finished and takes a look at her face, he swears he's never coming back, but in a couple of days he decides that he can't live without her."

Laughing, Gideon patted Finnie on the back. "Something like that I guess. Go spend some time with your family – you deserve it. I'll see you in a day or two."

As Gideon neared the jail, he spotted Doc and Zack sitting on the bench out front, leaning back, and smoking cigars. Both men were too preoccupied in their pleasures to notice the sheriff's approach.

Doc's arm was no longer in a sling, but he still walked with the cane. Mary and Zack had both noticed that the doctor didn't really put his weight on the walking stick, but Doc seemed to take solace in having it handy.

Noticing the cane resting between Doc's legs, Gideon called out, "Did you get infirm while I was gone?"

The two men looked towards Gideon in surprise.

"I got shot while you were gone is what I got," Doc stated.

Taken aback by the doctor's reply, Gideon rubbed his scar and took a deep breath that he exhaled loudly. "Finnie and I figured from those telegrams that something went on here. Shall we retire inside so that you two can catch me up on all that has happened?" he asked.

Gideon held the door open as Doc and Zack walked into the jail. Zack, out of habit, walked towards the sheriff's chair before realizing the mistake and altered his route to a seat in front of the desk. Doc sat down beside him.

"I'm almost afraid to hear what you two have to say, but I guess the good news is that I know you're both alive. Let's hear it," Gideon said.

Doc and Zack took turns telling Gideon all that had happened from their perspective. Each would interrupt to fill in details that the other left out. Both were determined to make sure Gideon knew all the facts. The doctor watched Gideon's face as they talked to try to determine the sheriff's reaction to the news. Gideon wasn't showing any response to what he heard, but he rubbed his scar so much that the skin was turning red. Knowing that Gideon tended to be a perfectionist with a very high opinion of his own abilities as a lawman, Doc wondered if the sheriff would think that Zack had failed at his duties.

After finishing telling all that had happened, Zack said, "Gideon, I'm truly sorry. I feel as if I let you and the town down. Things could have been handled a lot better."

The doctor tried to guess what was going on in Gideon's mind. The sheriff gazed blankly at Zack and then he turned his head and looked Doc right in the eye. Doc thought about winking to give Gideon a sign to take it easy, but decided better of it. He wanted to see how Gideon would react on his own, and if need be, he'd put the sheriff in his place. It wouldn't be the first time or probably the last.

Gideon didn't say anything, but stood up and walked to the washstand where he retrieved three coffee cups. He set them on the desk before sitting down and digging through his drawer until he found the bottle of tequila that Antonio Cortez had given him. After pulling the cork out with his teeth, he poured a generous amount of tequila into each cup and shoved two of them towards Doc and Zack.

"Gentlemen, I want to make a toast to a job well done. I don't think I could have done any better if I tried," Gideon said before clinking his glass with the other two.

Neither Doc nor Zack had ever before tasted the liquor. Doc licked his lips after taking a sip. Zack's cheeks and mouth puckered and he squinted his eyes.

"This stuff will grow on you," Gideon said.

"I already like it," Doc said and looked over at Zack. The young man had sat up straight in his chair and already looked as if the weight of the world had been lifted off his shoulders.

"It's certainly different," Zack said.

"Is your family still here?" Gideon asked Doc.

"No, they went home," Doc said with a little sadness in his voice.

"And you didn't go with them."

"No, I decided that my place is here."

"I see. You're going to make one little Irishman very happy," Gideon said.

"Don't remind me. He'll probably think that I stayed just to spend time with him," Doc groused.

"We wouldn't want anybody to think that you enjoyed his company," Gideon teased.

"Aren't you going to tell us about your trip?" Doc asked Gideon to change the subject.

Draining the rest of the tequila from his cup, Gideon said, "I will some other time. Gentlemen, I'm going home to see my wife and kids."

"There's a telegram and something from the banker on your desk," Zack said.

Digging through the stack of accumulated papers, Gideon found a telegram from Sheriff Henry. It read "Lester Cole guilty. Sentenced to hang." Scrounging around some more, he finally found a deposit slip from the bank. His account had been credited with a thousand dollars from Shad Nelson. Grinning, Gideon tossed the paper on the desk. The bounty hunter had been good on his word to Finnie and him on sending their share of the bounty.

"I didn't think this day could get any better after finding out that I'd never have to deal with Cyrus Capello ever again, but it just did. I got some stories to tell later," Gideon said.

Gideon walked down to the livery stable. He told Blackie that he would settle up with him later and borrowed a horse. As he headed out of town, Gideon felt giddy with anticipation. He gave the horse free rein and the animal took off in a lope.

Winnie and Chance were playing in the yard as Gideon rode up. They came running as he climbed off the horse. He squatted down and they ran into his arms, knocking him onto his butt. As they showered him with kisses, he tried to get a look at the children. Chance seemed to have grown a foot and had run off some of his baby fat. Winnie's face was changing from that of a pretty child into an awkward looking adolescent.

"I didn't think you'd ever make it home," Abby yelled from the porch as she came running.

Gideon stood as Abby ran into his arms. He lifted her off the ground and swung her in a circle.

"Sometimes it felt as if I'd never make it back," Gideon said before giving his wife a big kiss.

After all the greetings were exhausted and Winnie and Chance had caught Gideon up on their summer, he and Abby sat down on the swing.

"I talked to Doc and Zack. Sounds like things were exciting around here," Gideon said.

"That they were," Abby replied

"So how is everybody and everything?"

"Pretty darn good. The kids have had a good summer. They've missed you terribly. I think Winnie even more than Chance.   Sometimes it's hard to remember that there was a time when she couldn't stand you. Joann seems like her old self. She told me the other day that she's ready to have another baby. It made me cry. Ethan and Sarah adopted Sylvia, and of course, Benjamin is still Benjamin," Abby said with a laugh. "The herd is doing fine. Hiring String is the best thing we ever did for the ranch. That man has cattle ranching in his blood. He sees things and comes up with ideas that I never would have thought of, but I'm learning. We're going to have one of the finest herds in all of Colorado in a couple of years."

"Nobody told me what happened to Fancy," Gideon noted.

"She's still at the cabin with String."

"Really?   I can't imagine her being satisfied out there."

"She really is. I don't know what's going on with them. You know String – he doesn't say anything. I'll ask him if Fancy is still at the cabin and he'll say, 'Yup, she still there.' and that's as far as the conversation goes. But I can't imagine that Fancy is staying way out there just because she's fell in love with nature," Abby said and laughed.

"Wow, that would make for one mismatched couple. Whatever makes them happy."

"By the way, where is Buck?" Abby asked.

Looking towards the barn, Gideon paused for a moment. "Buck is dead. He got shot out from under me."

"Oh, Gideon, I know what that horse meant to you. I'm sorry."

"I know. Things won't be the same without him. That was one fine horse that I'm going to miss for a long time. I've been thinking that maybe I'll go catch me a young mustang. I've always admired Ethan's Pie. That is one sure-footed Indian pony. I could ride some of our horses until I got the mustang trained. It wouldn't seem like I'm replacing Buck as much that way. We'll see."

"Are you going to tell me about your trip?" Abby asked.

"We killed and caught the men that killed Rory. They killed a deputy and the one that survived is going to hang," Gideon replied.

Pausing as if she were almost afraid to ask, Abby said, "What about the family of the boy?"

Gideon let out a sigh. "I found them. The boy's name was Peter Irby. They forgave me," Gideon said quietly.

"Aren't you going to tell me more?" Abby inquired.

"Oh, I will some other day. The main thing is that they forgave me and it's over. After all these years, I have no reason left to feel guilty. I need to live a good life from now on. That's the last atonement I ever want to have to make," Gideon said.

Abby laid her head against Gideon's shoulder. "Oh, Mr. Johann, after the kids go to sleep time tonight you are going to be making all kinds of atonement," she said with a giggle.

About the Author

Duane Boehm is a musician, songwriter, and author. He lives on a mini-farm with his wife and an assortment of dogs. Having written short stories throughout his lifetime, he shared them with friends and with their encouragement began his journey as a novelist. Please feel free to email him at boehmduane@gmail.com or like his Facebook Page www.facebook.com/DuaneBoehmAuthor.

Made in the USA
Middletown, DE
05 March 2021

34874380R00132